ONE WAY

& OTHER STORIES

Other Titles from
Space Cowboy Books

Books:

Life During the Lazarus Age – Robert Frazier

Dreaming of Autonomous Vehicles – Jaroslav Olša, Jr.

The Future is Brief – Jean-Paul L. Garnier

Wave IX – Various Authors

The Martians - Emilie Procházková

Mexicans on the Moon – Pedro Iniguez

Another Time: Time Travel Stories 1942–1960

Complete Poems 1965–2020 – Michael Butterworth

Simultaneous Times Vol. 3 – Various Authors

Simultaneous Times Vol. 2.5 – Various Authors

Simultaneous Times Vol. 2 – Various Authors

Simultaneous Times Vol. 1 – Various Authors

Garbage In, Gospel Out – Jean-Paul L. Garnier

Betelgeuse Dimming – Jean-Paul L. Garnier

Future Anthropology – Jean-Paul L. Garnier

Chapbooks:

The Reducing Flame – Richard Magahiz

Micropoetry for Microplanets – Brian U. Garrison

Shelf Life – F. J. Bergmann

Mars Maundering – Denise Dumars

The Telepathy Machine – Jean-Paul L. Garnier

Time's Arrow – Jean-Paul L. Garnier

Utopian Problems – Jean-Paul L. Garnier

www.spacecowboybooks.com

ONE WAY

& OTHER STORIES

MIRIAM ALLEN DEFORD

ISBN: 978-1-968958-90-9

First Edition | 2025

Space Cowboy Books

61871 29 Palms Hwy.
Joshua Tree, CA 92252
www.spacecowboybooks.com

Table of Contents

Introduction
by Marie Vibbert

I was working as a software developer for a university library, and one of the archivists, knowing I was a writer of science fiction, invited me to view their collection of pulp magazines. Once admitted to the temperature-and-humidity-controlled sanctum, cotton-gloved, I gawped in excitement at the sepia and faded four-color spines, going back to the 1920s, while my librarian friend beamed proudly behind me. I reverently pulled a random issue from the early side of the collection down – careful to, as instructed, gently push in the issues on either side so I could grip the spine firmly and without damaging it. I turned it over in my hand and found, to my delight, a woman's name on the cover. I don't remember the issue date or the magazine, but I do remember the name. A woman I had never heard of: Miriam Allen deFord.

I had assumed the received wisdom that women simply didn't appear in these magazines, or did so only under male pseudonyms, but the evidence was right there, on the very first volume I ever held. This started me on a five-year-long project exploring the incidence of female name credits in science fiction magazines over time. I wanted to see how complex, how nonlinear the story of gender inclusion was, and I indeed found peaks and valleys, decades of joy like the 1990s and decades of backlash like the 2000s, but what I really discovered as I flipped through magazine after magazine was the vast wealth of foremothers I had, and how *good* they were. When a story jumped out at me for its vibrance, its originality, or its characters, it was almost always by a woman. Yet, in my youthful reading of short story collections, I found only the same one or two stories by women reprinted, ("That Only a Mother" by Judith Merril before 1975 and Le Guin's "Those Who Walk Away from Omelas" after 1975). The editors seemed to think that having had one story by a woman, they could not possibly have another, the bulk of their collections taken up by the same four or five men. Men who, no offense, were not as good. (A notable exception being Ray Bradbury.) Women in

SF were doing what Bradbury was praised for, long before he did: bringing literary realism to the genre.

It's not surprising that deFord's was the name I caught in that random pull. She was famously prolific. From her first in 1928 to her last in 1978, she published over 90 stories in American pulp magazines, many of which would go on to be translated into French, German, Croatian, and other languages. She was one of the "monstrous horde of women" Heinlein accused Anthony Boucher of publishing. (The "horde" was, in fact, at its peak only 10% of F&SF's bylines, but that was more than double the percentage of writers writing under female names in other magazines during Boucher's tenure: 1949 to 1958.)

Boucher deserves the backhanded compliment. He sought out the best writers, period, without regard to what they had under their clothes. It was Boucher's openness to mystery and crime in F&SF that led deFord to his magazine and from there to branch out from her start in nonfiction, mystery and crime stories. Not that she would ever leave crime and mystery, editing multiple anthologies of crime fiction, including one of SF crime stories titled *Space, Time, and Crime* in 1964 and producing nonfiction books like *Murders Sane & Mad* in 1965. Her book about a murder during the time of James the First, *The Overbury Affair,* won the Mystery Writers of America's Edgar Award in 1961 for Best Fact Crime. Get a taste for her fondness for a good murder in this collection with "The Akkra Case" or "Time Out for Redheads."

It is not safe to be a protagonist in Ms. deFord's stories, but she never punches down, and is frequently funny. She'll destroy humanity and leave you with a smirk and a wink. Most notably in the devastating last two lines of "Margenes." I'll leave you to discover that one.

She is often in direct conversation with the genre's tropes. What if the wife is smarter than her husband? What if the working everyman catches on to the alien? Was 1961's "Oh, Rats!" a response to "Flowers for Algernon" which won the Hugo for best short story the year before? (I can see her shaking her head over her F&SF issue, "A rat would never be that nice. Where's my pen?")

"One Way" stood out to me for the confident way it builds its world without waiting for the reader – tossing neologisms and simple sentences that turn notions on their heads. "Beard Removal Center" and "Cybernetics Approval Slip" are dropped without explanation. One is easy to interpret, the other less so. "They let us start a child," alerts us to a world of overpopulation (four billion! Sadly, half the population we have today was a dark vision in 1955.) Then, for no reason I can fathom, we have thirteen months? Well, why take even calendars for granted?

There's a freeness and a daring to her leaps of language. Her characters hit an "autocaf" and watch the "tridemens," where other authors would have relied on already-coined terms like "automat" and "holographic TV." "Mobileways" edged with a "stand-pave" throw us into a new world that feels grown out of our own, like the slang of a new generation. Hell, get really out there and play some "phph" for a "ganath" or so and have some "mastonyi" to celebrate.

Her futures are never quite utopias nor dystopias. They are simply different. She sees humanity solving some problems, persisting with others, making up all new ones. She sees and notices class divisions, be they between workers and administrators or winged and ground-dwelling aliens.

Miriam Allen deFord was an activist, a socialist, a suffragette and a WPA writer. She made no secret of her political and social opinions, stating in an interview, "I am unalterably and actively opposed to fascism, Nazism, Hitlerism, Hirohitoism, or whatever name may be applied to the monster."[1] If the social mores in her stories feel not quite so clearly leftist, remember the prevailing conservatism of the Golden Age that they were up against, and perhaps the influence of editorial staff anxious to not get blacklisted. It's rare to see stories in this era where the working characters aren't the rubes there to be talked down to by the scientist-protagonist. (Looking at you, Asimov.)

---

[1] Writers take sides: letters about the war in Spain from 418 American authors. League of American writers, New York, (1938), pp. 18-19.

All of deFord's characters *work*.

It's exceptional to see early pulp stories where women have ideas at all, much less solve problems. Even female-identifying writers of the time often did not give their characters the full agency they would have applied to themselves. (Perhaps feeling that they were "not like the other girls?") Miriam Allen deFord lets women think, and act, and engage in daring-do.

But what I admire most about Miriam Allen deFord is that beyond the page she was a woman of conviction. She was a socialist when socialism was a fresh idea, before 1920, and also active at the same time in women's suffrage. She distributed birth control and campaigned for its use and wrote for leftist newspapers and magazines. Born to a world where women could not own property, she saw a future that was different and worked to create it. No wonder she could so easily see the different worlds her descendants might devise.

Not Snow, Nor Rain

On his first day as a mail carrier, Sam Wilson noted that inscription, cribbed from Herodotus, on the General Post Office, and took it to heart: "Not snow, nor rain, nor heat, nor gloom of night stays these couriers from the swift completion of their appointed rounds."

It couldn't be literally true, of course. Given a real blizzard, it would be impossible to make his way through the pathless drifts; and if there had been a major flood, he could hardly have swum to deliver letters to the marooned. Moreover, if he couldn't find the addressee, there was nothing to do but mark the envelope "Not known at this address," and take it back to be returned to the addresser or consigned to the Dead Letter Office. But through the years, Sam Wilson had been as consciously faithful and efficient as any Persian messenger.

Now the long years had galloped by, and this was the very last time he would walk his route before his retirement.

It would be good to put his feet up somewhere and ease them back into comfort; they had been Sam's loyal servants and they were more worn out than he was. But the thought of retirement bothered him. Mollie was going to get sick of having him around the house all day, and he was damned if he was going to sit on a park bench like other discarded old men and suck a pipe and stare at nothing, waiting for the hours to pass in a vacuum. He had his big interest, of course—his status as a devoted science fiction fan; he would have time now to read and reread, to watch hopefully from the roof of his apartment house for signs of a flying saucer. But that wasn't enough; what he needed was a project to keep him alert and occupied.

On his last delivery he found it.

The Ochterlonie Building, way down on lower Second Avenue, was a rundown, shabby old firetrap, once as solid as the Scotsman who had built it and named it for himself, but now, with its single open-cage elevator and its sagging floors, attracting only quack doctors and dubious private eyes and similar fauna on the edge of free enterprise.

Sam had been delivering to it now for 35 years, watching its slow deterioration.

This time there was a whole batch of self-addressed letters for a tenant whose name was new to him, but that was hardly surprising—nowadays, in the Ochterlonie Building, tenants came and went.

They were small envelopes, addressed in blue, in printing simulating handwriting, to Orville K. Hesterson, Sec.-Treas., Time-Between-Time, 746 Ochterlonie Building, New York 3, N. Y. Feeling them with experienced fingers, Sam Wilson judged they were orders for something, doubtless enclosing money.

•

In most of the buildings on his last route, Sam knew, at least by sight, the employees who took in the mail, and they knew him. A lot of them knew this was his last trip; there were farewells and good wishes, and even a few small donations (since he wouldn't be there next Christmas) which he gratefully tucked in an inside pocket of the uniform he would never wear again. There were also two or three invitations to a drink, which, being still on duty, he had regretfully to decline.

But in the Ochterlonie Building, with its fly-by-night clientele, he was just the postman, and nobody greeted him except Howie Mallory, the decrepit elevator operator. Sam considered him soberly. It was going to be pretty tough financially from now on; could he, perhaps, find a job like Howie's? No. Not unless things got a lot tougher; standing all day would be just as bad as walking.

He went from office to office, getting rid of his load—mostly bills, duns and complaints, he imagined, in this hole. There was nothing for the seventh floor except this bunch for Time-Between-Time.

The seventh floor? He must be nuts. The Ochterlonie Building was six floors high.

Puzzled, he rang for Howie.

"What'd they do, build a penthouse office on top of this old dump?" he inquired.

The elevator operator laughed as at a feeble jest. "Sure," he said airily. "General Motors is using it as a hideaway."

"No, Howie—no fooling. Look here."

Mallory stared and shook his head. "There ain't no 746. Somebody got the number wrong. Or they got the building wrong. There's nobody here by that name."

"They couldn't—printed envelopes like these."

"O. K., wise guy," said Howie. "Look for yourself."

He led the way to the short flight of iron stairs and the trap door. While Mallory stood jeering at him, Sam determinedly climbed through. There was nothing in sight but the plain flat roof. He climbed down again.

"Last letters on my last delivery and I can't deliver them," Sam Wilson said disgustedly.

"Somebody's playing a joke, maybe."

"Crazy joke. Well, so long, Howie. Some young squirt will be taking his life in his hands in this broken-down cage of yours tomorrow."

Sam Wilson, whom nothing could deter from the swift completion of his appointed rounds, had to trudge back to the post office with 22 undelivered letters.

Years ago the United States Post Office gave up searching directories and reference books, or deciphering illiterate or screwy addresses, so as to make every possible delivery. That went out with three daily and two Saturday deliveries, two-cent drop postage, and all the other amenities that a submissive public let itself lose without a protest. But there was still a city directory in the office. Sam Wilson searched it stubbornly. Time-Between-Time was not listed. Neither was Orville K. Hesterson. There was nothing to do but consider the letters nixies and turn them over to the proper department. If there was another bunch of them tomorrow, he would never know.

•

Retirement, after the first carefree week, was just as bad as Sam Wilson had suspected it was going to be. Not bad enough to think yet about elevator operating or night watching, but bad enough to make him restless and edgy, and to make him snap Mollie's head off until they had their first bad quarrel for years. He'd never had time enough before to keep up with all the science fiction magazines and books. Now, with nothing but time, there weren't enough of them to fill the long days. What he needed was something—something that didn't involve walking—to make those endless hours speed up. He began thinking again about those 22 nixies.

He sat gloomily on a bench in Tompkins Square in the spring sunshine: just what he had sworn not to do, but if he stayed home another hour, Mollie would heave the vacuum cleaner at him. In the public library he had searched directories and phone books, for all the boroughs and for suburban New Jersey, Connecticut and Pennsylvania; Orville K. Hesterson appeared in none of them.

He didn't know why it was any of his business, except that Time-Between-Time had put a blot on the very end of his 35-year record and he wanted revenge. Also, it was something to do and be interested in. In a way, science fiction and detection had a lot in common, and Sam Wilson prided himself on his ability to guess ahead what was going to happen in a story. So why couldn't he figure out this puzzle, right here in Manhattan, Terra? But he was stymied.

Or was he?

Sam took his gloomy thoughts to Mulligan's. Every large city is a collection of villages. The people who live long enough in a neighborhood acquire their own groceries, their own drugstores, their own bars. The Wilsons had lived six years in their flat, and Mulligan's, catercornered across the street, was Sam's personal bar.

He was cautious as to what he said there. He'd heard enough backtalk already when he had been indiscreet enough once, after four beers, to express his views on UFOs. He had no desire to gain a reputation as a crackpot. But it was safe enough to remark conversationally, "How do you find out where a guy is when he says he's someplace and you write him there and the letter comes back?"

"You ought to know, Sam," said Ed, the day barkeep. "You were a postman long enough."

"If I knew, I wouldn't ask."

"Ask Information on the phone."

"He hasn't got a phone." That was the weirdest part of it—a business office without a phone.

In every bar, at every moment, there is somebody who knows all the answers. This somebody, a nondescript fellow nursing a Collins down the bar, spoke up: "It could be unlisted."

Sam's acquaintance didn't include people with unlisted phones; he hadn't thought of that.

"Then how do you find out his number?"

"You don't, unless he tells you. That's why he has it unlisted."

The police could get it, Sam thought. But they wouldn't, without a reason.

"Hey, maybe this guy's office is in one of them flying saucers and he forgot to come down and get his mail," Ed suggested brightly.

Sam scowled and walked out.

Nevertheless....

Nothing to do with UFOs, of course. That was ridiculous.

•

But suppose there was a warp in the space-time continuum? Suppose there had once been another Ochterlonie Building, or some day in the future there was going to be another one, somewhere in New York? There wasn't another now, in any of the boroughs, or any other building with a name remotely like it; his research had already established that. Sam went back to the Public Library. The building he knew had been erected in 1898. He consulted directories as far back as they went; there never had been one of the name before. Then a time-slip from the future? That was hopeless, so far as he could do anything about it, so he cast about for another solution. How about a parallel world?

That could be, certainly: some accident by which mail for that other Ochterlonie Building, the seven-story one, had (maybe just once) arrived in the wrong dimension.

He couldn't do anything to prove or disprove that, either. What he needed was a break.

He got it.

One morning in early summer his own mailbox in the downstairs hallway disgorged a long envelope, addressed to Mr. Samuel Wilson. The upper left-hand corner bore a printed return address: Time-Between-Time, 746 Ochterlonie Building, New York 3, N. Y. He raced upstairs, locked himself in the bathroom, the one place Mollie couldn't interrupt him, and tore the envelope open with trembling fingers.

It was a form letter, with the "Dear Mr. Wilson" not too accurately typed in. It enclosed one of those blue-printed envelopes in simulated handwriting. The letterhead carried the familiar impossible address, but no phone number.

Maybe it was chance, maybe it was ESP, but he himself had got onto Time-Between-Time's mailing list!

•

He had trouble focusing his eyes to read the letter.

Dear Mr. Wilson:

Would you invest $1 to get a chance at $1,000?

Of course you would, especially if, win or lose, you got your dollar back.

In this atomic age, yesterday's science fiction has become today's and tomorrow's science fact. Time-Between-Time, a new organization, is planning establishment of a publishing company to bring out the best in new books, both fact and fiction, in the field of science, appealing to people who have never been interested until now.

Before we start, we are conducting a poll to find out what the general public thinks and feels about our probabilities of success. We're asking for your co-operation.

Our statisticians have told us that from the answers to one question—which may look off the beam but isn't—we can make a pretty good estimate. Here it is:

If tomorrow morning a spaceship landed in front of your house, and from it issued a band of extraterrestrial beings, who might or might not be human in appearance, what, in your best judgment, would be your own immediate reaction? Check one, or if you agree with none of the choices, indicate in the blank space beneath what your personal reaction would probably be.

1. Phone for the police. 2. Attack the aliens physically. 3. Faint. 4. Run away. 5. Call for assistance to seize the visitors. 6. Greet them, attempt to communicate, and welcome them in the name of your fellow-terrestrials. 7. Other (please specify).

Return this letter, properly marked, in the enclosed envelope. To defray promotion expenses, enclose a dollar bill (no checks or money orders). At the conclusion of this poll, all answers will be evaluated. The writer of the one which comes nearest to the answer reached by our electronic computer, which will be fed the same question, will receive $1,000 in dollar bills. Ties will receive duplicate prizes.

In addition, all participants, when our publishing firm has been established, will receive for their $1 a credit form entitling them to $1 off any book we publish.

Don't delay. Send in your answer NOW. Only letters enclosing $1 will be entered.

Very truly yours,

Time-Between-Time,

Orville K. Hesterson,

Sec.-Treas.

•

Sam Wilson read the letter three times. "It's crazy," he muttered. "It's a gyp."

What he ought to do was take the letter to the post office—Mr. Gross would be the one to see—and let them decide whether this Hesterson was using the mails to defraud. Let Mr. Gross and his department try to find 746 in the six-story Ochterlonie Building. As a faithful employee for 35 years, it was Sam's plain duty.

But then it would be out of his hands forever; he'd never even find out what happened. And he'd be back in the dull morass that retirement was turning out to be.

"Sam!" Mollie yelled outside the locked door. "Aren't you ever coming out of there?"

"I'm coming, I'm coming!" He put the letter and its enclosure back in the envelope and placed them in a pocket.

Time enough to decide that afternoon what he was going to do.

He escaped after lunch to what was becoming his refuge on a park bench. There he read the letter for the fourth time. For a long while he sat ruminating. About three o'clock he walked to the General Post Office—walking had become a habit hard to break—and hunted up the man who now had his old route, a youngster not more than 30 named Flanagan.

From the letter Sam extracted the return envelope.

"You been delivering any like this?" he asked.

Flanagan peered at it.

"Yeah," he said. "Plenty." He looked worried. "Gee, Wilson, I'm glad you came in. There's something funny about those deliveries, and I don't want to get in Dutch."

"Funny how?"

"My very first day on the route, I started up to the seventh floor of that building to deliver them—and there wasn't any seventh floor. So I asked the old elevator man—"

"Howie Mallory. I know him. He's been there for years."

"I guess so. Anyway, he said it was O. K. just to give them to him. He showed me a paper, signed with the name of this outfit, by the secretary or something—"

"Orville K. Hesterson," Sam said.

"That was it—saying that all mail for them was to be delivered to the elevator operator until further notice. So I've been giving it to him ever since—there's a big bunch every day. Is something wrong, Sam? Have I pulled a boner? Am I going to be in trouble?"

"No trouble. I'm just checking—little job they asked me to do for them, seeing I'm retired." Sam was surprised at the glibness with which that fib came out.

Flanagan looked still more worried. "He said their office was being remodeled or something, so he was looking after their mail till they could move in."

"Sure. Don't give it another thought." Another idea occurred to him; he lowered his voice. "I oughtn't to tell you this, Flanagan, but every new man on a route, they kind of check up on him the first few weeks, see if he's handling everything O.K. I'll tell them you're doing fine."

"Hey, thanks. Thanks a lot."

"Don't say anything about this. It's supposed to be secret."

"Oh, I won't."

Sam Wilson waved and walked out. He sat on the steps a while to think. Was old Howie Mallory pulling a fast one? Was *he* Orville K. Hesterson? Had he cooked up a scheme to make himself some crooked money?

•

Three things against that. First, those nixies the first day: why wouldn't Mallory have told him the same thing he told Flanagan? Sam would have believed him, if he had said they were building an office on the roof and giving it a number.

Second, Howie just wasn't smart enough. Of course he could be fronting for the real crook. But Sam had known him for years, and old Howie had always seemed downright stupidly honest. A man doesn't suddenly turn into a criminal after a lifetime of probity.

Third, if this was some fraudulent scheme involving Mallory, nobody the old man knew—least of all the postman who used to deliver mail to that very building—would ever have been allowed to appear on the sucker list.

Sam Wilson thought some more. Then he hunted up the nearest pay phone and called Mollie.

"Mollie? Sam. Look, I just met an old friend of mine—" he picked a name from a billboard visible from the phone booth—"Bill Seagram, you remember him—oh, sure you do; you've just forgotten. Anyway, he's just here for the day and we're going to have dinner and see a show. Don't wait up for me. I might be pretty late.... No, I'm *not* phoning from Mulligan's.... Now you know me, Mollie; do I ever drink too much?... Yeah, sure, he ought to've asked you too, but he didn't. O.K., he's impolite. Aw, Mollie, don't be like that—"

She hung up on him.

Sam Wilson stood concealed in a doorway from which he could see the cramped lobby of the Ochterlonie Building. It was ten minutes before somebody entered it and rang for the elevator. The minute Howie Mallory started up with his passenger, Sam darted into the building and started climbing the stairs. He heard Mallory passing him, going down again, but the elevator wasn't visible from the stairway. On the sixth floor, after a quick survey to see that the hall was clear and the doors closed that he had to pass, he found the iron steps to the trapdoor.

The roof was just as empty as the other time he had visited it. No, it wasn't. In a corner by the parapet, weighted with a brick to keep it from blowing away, was a large paper bag. Sam picked up the brick and looked inside. It was stuffed with those blue-printed return envelopes.

He looked carefully about him. There were buildings all around, towering over the little old Ochterlonie Building. There were plenty of windows from which a curious eye could discern anything happening on that roof. But at night anybody in those buildings would be either working late or cleaning offices, with no reason whatever to go to a window; and Sam was sure nothing was going to happen till after dark. It was a warm day and he had been carrying his coat. He folded it and put it down near the paper bag and sat on it with his back against the parapet. He cursed himself for not having had more foresight; he should have brought something to eat and something to read. Well, he wasn't going to climb down all those stairs and up again. He lighted his pipe and began waiting.

He must have dozed off, for he came to himself with a start and found it was almost dark. The paper bag was still there. It was just as well he had slept; now he'd have no trouble staying awake and watching. He might very well be there all night—in fact, he'd have to be, whether anything happened or not. The front door would be locked by now. Mollie would have a fit, but he had his alibi ready.

There was only one explanation left. Not time travel. Not alternate universes. Not an ordinary confidence game. Not—decidedly not—a hoax.

If he was wrong, then tomorrow morning he'd take the whole business to Mr. Gross. But he had a hunch he wasn't going to be wrong.

•

It was 12:15 by his wristwatch when he saw it coming.

It had no lights; nobody could have spotted it as it appeared suddenly out of nowhere and climbed straight down. It landed lightly as a drop of dew. The port opened and a small, spare man, very neatly dressed, as Sam could see with eyes accustomed to the darkness, stepped out. Orville K. Hesterson in person.

He tiptoed quickly to the paper bag. Then he saw Sam and stopped short. Sam reached out and grabbed a wrist. It felt like flesh, but he couldn't be sure.

"Who are you? What are you doing here?" the newcomer said in a strained whisper, just like a scared character in a soap opera. So he spoke English. Good: Sam didn't speak anything else.

"I'm from the United States Post Office," Sam replied suavely. Well, he had been, long enough, hadn't he?

"Oh. Well, now look, my friend—"

"*You* look. Talk. How much are you paying the elevator operator to put your mail up here every day?"

"Five dollars a day, in dollar bills, six days a week, left in the empty bag," answered Hesterson—it must be Hesterson—sullenly. "That's no crime, is it? Call this my office, and call that my rent. All I need an office for is to have somewhere to get my letters."

"Letters with money in them."

"We have to have funds for postage, don't we?"

"What about the postage on the first mailing list, before you got any dollars to pay for stamps?"

If it had been a little lighter, Sam would have been surer of the alarm that crossed Hesterson's face.

"I—well, we had to fabricate some of your currency for that. We regretted it—we aim to obey all local rules and regulations. As soon as we have enough coming in, we intend to send the amount to the New York postmaster as anonymous conscience money."

"How about the $1,000 prize? And those dollar book credits?"

"Oh, that. Well, we say '*when* our publishing firm has been established,' don't we? That publishing thing is just a gimmick. As for the $1,000, we give no intimation of when the poll will end."

Sam tightened his grasp on the wrist, which was beginning to wriggle.

"I see. O.K., explain the whole setup. It sounds crazy to me."

"I couldn't agree with you more," said Mr. Hesterson, to Sam's surprise. "That's exactly what, in our own idiom, I told—" Sam couldn't get the name; it sounded like a grunt. "But he's the boss and I'm only a scout third class." His voice grew plaintive. "You can't imagine what an ordeal it is, almost every week, to have to land in a secluded place where I can hide the flyer, make my way to New York, and buy a bunch of stamps and mail a batch of letters in broad daylight. We can simulate your paper and printing and typing well enough, but"—that grunt again—"insists we use genuine stamps. I told you we try to follow all your laws, as far as we possibly can. It's very difficult for me to keep this absurd shape for long at a time; I'm exhausted after every trip. I can assure you, these little night excursions from the mother-ship to pick up the letters are the very least of my burdens!"

"What in time does your boss think he's going to gain by such a screwy come-on?"

"'In time'? Oh, just an idiomatic phrase. Like our calling our organization Time-Between-Time, time of course being just a dimension of space. I learned your tongue mostly from the B.B.C. and I don't always understand your speech in New York. My dear sir, do you here on this planet ask your bosses why they concoct their plans? Mine has a very profound mind; that's why he is the boss. All I know is that he persuaded the Council to try it out. A softening-up process—isn't that what you people call it when you use it in your silly wars with one another?"

"Softening for what?" But Sam Wilson knew the answer already.

•

"Why, for the invasion, of course," said Orville K. Hesterson, whose own name was probably a grunt. "Surely you must be aware that, with planetwide devastation likely and even imminent, every world whose inhabitants can live comfortably under extreme radiation is looking to yours—Earth, as you call it—as a possible area for colonization? So many planets are so terribly overcrowded—there's always a rush for a new frontier. We've missed out too often; this time we're determined to be first."

"I'll be darned," said Sam, "if I can see how that questionnaire would be any help to you."

"But it's elementary, as I believe one of your famous law-enforcers once declared. First of all, we're gaining a pretty good idea of what kind of reception we're likely to meet when we arrive, and therefore whether we're going to need weapons to destroy what will be left of the population, or can reasonably expect to take over without difficulty. We figure that a cross-section of one of your largest cities will be a pretty good indication, and we can extrapolate from that. In the second place, the question itself is deliberately worded to startle the recipients, who have never in their lives contemplated such a thing as an extraterrestrial visitor—"

"Not me. I'm a science fiction fan from way back. It's all old stuff to me."

Hesterson clicked his tongue—or at least the tongue he was wearing. "Oh, dear, that *was* an error. We tried particularly not to include on our lists subscribers to any of your speculative periodicals. That wasn't my mistake, thank goodness; it was another scout who had the horrible job of spending several days here and compiling the lists. Under your present low radioactivity it's real agony for us."

"I'll tell you one mistake you did make, though," said Sam angrily. "You ought to've arranged with the elevator man before your first lot of answers was due. If you want to know, that's how I got onto the whole thing. I'm a mail carrier—I'm retired now, but I was then—and I was the one supposed to deliver the first batch. Mallory—that's the elevator operator—laughed in my face and told me there wasn't any 746 in this building, and I had to take the letters back to the post office—on my *last* delivery!" Sam couldn't keep the bitterness out of his voice. "After 35 years—well, that's neither here nor there. But I didn't like that and I made up my mind to find out what was happening."

"So that's it. Oh, dear, dear. I'll have to compensate for that or I *will* be in trouble."

Sam had had enough. "You are in trouble right now," he growled, pushing the little alien back against the parapet. "We're staying right here till morning, and then I'm going to call for help and take you and your flying saucer or whatever it is straight to the F.B.I."

The counterfeit Mr. Hesterson laughed.

"Oh, no indeed you aren't," he said mildly. "I can slip right back into my own shape whenever I want to—the only reason I haven't done it yet is that then I wouldn't have the equipment to talk to you—and I assure you that you couldn't hold me then. On the contrary. As you just pointed out to me, I did make one bad error, and my boss doesn't like errors. I have no intention of making another one by leaving you here to spread the news."

"What do you mean?" Sam Wilson cried. For the first time, after the years of accustomedness to the idea of extraterrestrial beings, a thrill of pure terror shot through him.

"This," said the outsider softly.

•

Before Sam could take another breath, the wrist he was holding slid from his grasp, all of Mr. Hesterson slithered into something utterly beyond imagining, and Sam found himself enveloped in invisible chains against which he was unable to make the slightest struggle. He felt himself being lifted and thrown into the cockpit. Something landed on top of him—undoubtedly the package of prize entries and dollar bills. His last conscious thought was a despairing one of Mollie.

Sam Wilson, devoted mail carrier, was making a longer trip than any Persian courier ever dreamed of, and not snow, nor rain, nor heat, nor gloom of night could stay him from his appointed round.

But he may not be gone forever. If he can be kept alive on that planet in some other solar system, they plan to bring him back as Exhibit One whenever World War III has made Earth sufficiently radioactive for Orville K. Hesterson's co-planetarians to live here comfortably.

Oh, Rats!

SK540, the 27th son of two very ordinary white laboratory rats, surveyed his world.

He was no more able than any other rat to possess articulate speech, or to use his paws as hands. All he had was a brain which, relative to its size, was superior to any rat's that had hitherto appeared on Earth. It was enough.

In the first week of gestation his embryo had been removed to a more suitable receptacle than the maternal womb, and his brain had been stimulated with orthedrin, maxiton and glutamic acid. It had been continuously irrigated with blood. One hemisphere had been activated far in excess of the other, since previous experiments had shown that increased lack of symmetry between the hemispheres produced superior mentality. The end-result was an enormous increase in brain-cells in both hemispheres. His brain showed also a marked increase in cholinesterase over that of other rats.

SK540, in other words, was a super-rat.

The same processes had been applied to all his brothers and sisters. Most of them had died. The few who did not, failed to show the desired results, or showed them in so lopsided and partial a manner that it was necessary to destroy them.

All of this, of course had been mere preparation and experimentation with a view to later developments in human subjects. What SK540's gods had not anticipated was that they would produce a creature mentally the superior, not only of his fellow-rats, but also, in some respects, of themselves.

He was a super-rat: but he was still a rat. His world of dreams and aspirations was not human, but murine.

What would you do if you were a brilliant, moody young super-rat, caged in a laboratory?

SK540 did it.

What human beings desired was health, freedom, wealth, love, and power. So did SK540. But to him health was taken for granted; freedom was freedom from cages, traps, cats, and dogs; wealth meant shelter from cold and rain and plenty to eat; love meant a constant supply of available females.

But power! It was in his longing for power that he most revealingly displayed his status as super-rat.

Therefore, once he had learned how to open his cage, he was carefully selective of the companions—actually, the followers—whom he would release to join his midnight hegira from the laboratory. Only the meekest and most subservient of the males—intelligent but not too intelligent— and the most desirable and amiable of the females were invited.

Once free of the cages, SK540 had no difficulty in leading his troop out of the building. The door of the laboratory was locked, but a window was slightly open from the top. Rats can climb up or down.

Like a silver ribbon they flowed along the dark street, SK540, looking exactly like all the rest, at their head. Only one person in the deserted streets seems to have noticed them, and he did not understand the nature of the phenomenon.

•

Young Mr. and Mrs. Philip Vinson started housekeeping in what had once been a mansion. It was now a rundown eyesore.

It had belonged to Norah Vinson's great-aunt Martha, who had left it to her in her will. The estate was in litigation, but the executor had permitted the Vinsons to settle down in the house, though they weren't allowed yet to sell it. It had no modern conveniences, and was full of rooms they couldn't use and heavy old-fashioned furniture; but it was solidly built and near the laboratory where he worked as a technician, and they could live rent-free until they could sell the house and use the money to buy a real home.

"Something funny happened in the lab last night," Philip reported, watching Norah struggle with dinner on the massive coal-stove.

"Somebody broke in and stole about half our experimental animals. And they got our pride and joy."

"The famous SK540?" Norah asked.

"The same. Actually, it wasn't a break-in. It must have been an inside job. The cages were open but there were no signs of breaking and entering. We're all under suspicion till they find out who-dunit."

Norah looked alarmed.

"You too? What on earth would anybody want with a lot of laboratory rats? They aren't worth anything, are they—financially, I mean?"

"Not a cent. That's why I'm sure one of the clean-up kids must have done it. Probably wanted them for pets. They're all tame, of course, not like wild rats—though they can bite like wild rats if they want to. Some of the ones missing are treated, and some are controls. It would just be a nuisance if they hadn't taken SK540. Now they've got to find him, or do about five years' work over again, without any assurance of as great a success. To say nothing of letting our super-rat loose on the world."

"What on earth could even a super-rat do that would matter—to human beings, I mean?"

"Nobody knows. Maybe that's what we're going to find out."

•

That night Norah woke suddenly with a loud scream. Philip got the gas lighted—there was no electricity in the old house—and held her shaking body in his arms. She found her breath at last long enough to sob: "It was a rat! A rat ran right over my face!"

"You're dreaming, darling. It's because I told you about the theft at the lab. There couldn't be rats in this place. It's too solidly built, from the basement up."

He finally got her to sleep again, but he lay awake for a long time, listening. Nothing happened.

Rats can't talk, but they can communicate. About the time Norah Vinson dropped off after her frightened wakening, SK540 was confronting a culprit. The culprit was one of the liberated males. His beady eyes tried to gaze into the implacable ones of SK540, but his tail twitched nervously and if he bared his teeth it was more in terror than in fight. They all knew that strict orders had been given not to disturb the humans in the house until SK540 had all his preparations made.

A little more of that silent communication, and the rat who had run over Norah's face knew he had only two choices—have his throat slit or get out. He got.

"What do you know?" Philip said that evening. "One of our rats came back."

"By itself?"

"Yeah. I never heard of such a thing. It was one of the experimental ones, so it was smarter than most, though not such an awful lot. I never heard of a rat with homing instinct before. But when we opened up this morning, there he was, sitting in his cage, ready for breakfast."

"Speaking of breakfast, I thought I asked you to buy a big box of oatmeal on your way home yesterday. It's about the only thing in the way of cereal I can manage on that old stove."

"I did buy it. Don't you remember? I left it in the kitchen."

"Well, it wasn't there this morning. All I know is that you're going to have nothing but toast and coffee tomorrow. We seem to be out of eggs, too. And bacon. And I thought we had half a pound left of that cheese, but that's gone too."

"Good Lord, Norah, if you've got that much marketing to do, can't you do it yourself?"

"Sure, if you leave the car. I'm not going to walk all that way and back."

So of course Philip did do the shopping the next day. Besides, Norah had just remembered she had a date at the hairdresser's.

•

When he got home her hair was still uncurled and she was in hysterics. One of the many amenities great-aunt Martha's house lacked was a telephone; anyway, Norah couldn't have been coherent over one. She cast herself, shuddering and crying, into Philip's arms, and it was a long time before he got her soothed enough for her to gasp: "Philip! They wouldn't let me out!"

"They? Who? What do you mean?"

"The—the rats! The white rats. They made a ring around me at the front door so I couldn't open it. I ran to the back and they beat me there and did the same thing. I even tried the windows but it was no use. And their teeth—they all—I guess I went to pieces. I started throwing things at them and they just dodged. I yelled for help but there's nobody near enough to hear. Then I gave up and ran in our bedroom and slammed the door on them, but they left guards outside. I heard them squeaking till you drove up, then I heard them run away."

Philip stared at her, scared to death. His wife had lost her mind.

"Now, now, sweetheart," he said soothingly, "let's get this straight. They fired a lab boy today. They found four of our rats in his home. He told some idiotic story of having 'found' them, with the others missing, running loose on the street that night, but of course he stole them. He must have sold the rest of them to other kids; they're working on that now."

Norah blew her nose and wiped her eyes. She had regained her usual calm.

"Philip Vinson," she said coldly, "are you accusing me of lying, or just of being crazy? I'm neither. I saw and heard those rats. They're here *now*. What's more, I guess I know where that oatmeal went, and the eggs and bacon too, and the cheese. I'm—I'm a hostage!"

"I don't suppose," she added sarcastically, "that your SK540 was one of the ones they found in the boy's home?"

"No, it wasn't," he acknowledged uneasily. A nasty little icy trickle stole down his spine. "All right, Norah, I give in. You take the poker and I'll take the hammer, and we'll search this house from cellar to attic."

"You won't find them," said Norah bitterly. "SK540's too smart. They'll stay inside the walls and keep quiet."

"Then we'll find the holes they went through and rout them out."

They didn't, of course. There wasn't a sign of a rathole, or of a rat.

They got through dinner and the evening somehow. Norah put all the food not in cans inside the old-fashioned icebox which took the place of a refrigerator. Philip thought he was too disturbed to be able to sleep, but he did, and Norah, exhausted, was asleep as soon as her head touched the pillow.

His last doubt of his wife's sanity vanished when, the next morning, they found the icebox door open and half the food gone.

•

"That settles it!" Philip announced. "Come on, Norah, put your coat on. You're coming with me to the lab and we'll report what's happened.

They'll find those creatures if they have to tear the house apart to do it. That boy must have been telling the truth."

"You couldn't keep me away," Norah responded. "I'll never spend another minute alone in this house while those dreadful things are in it."

But of course when they got to the front door, there they were, circling them, their teeth bared. The same with the back door and all the first floor windows.

"That's SK540 all right, leading them," Philip whispered through clenched jaws. He could smash them all, he supposed, in time, with what weapons he had. But he worked in the laboratory. He knew their value to science, especially SK540's.

Rats couldn't talk, he knew, and they couldn't understand human speech. Nevertheless, some kind of communication might establish itself. SK540's eyes were too intelligent not to believe that he was getting the gist of talk directed to him.

"This is utterly ridiculous," Philip grated. "If you won't let us out, how can we keep bringing food into the house for you? We'll all starve, you and we together."

He could have sworn SK540 was considering. But he guessed the implicit answer. Let either one of them out, now they knew the rats were there, and men from the laboratory would come quickly and overwhelm and carry off the besiegers. It was a true impasse.

"Philip," Norah reminded him, "if you don't go to work, they know we haven't a phone, and somebody will be here pretty soon to find out if anything's wrong."

But that wouldn't help, Philip reflected gloomily; they'd let anyone in, and keep him there.

And he thought to himself, and was careful not to say it aloud: rats are rats. Even if they are 25th generation laboratory-born. When the other food was gone there would be human meat.

He did not want to look at them any more. He took Norah's arm and turned away into their bedroom.

They stayed there all day, too upset to think of eating, talking and talking to no conclusion. As dusk came on they did not light the gas. Exhausted, they lay down on the bed without undressing.

After a while there was a quiet scratching at the door.

"Don't let them in!" Norah whispered. Her teeth were chattering.

"I must, dear," he whispered back. "It isn't 'them,' I'm sure of it—it's just SK540 himself. I've been expecting him. We've got to reach some kind of understanding."

"With a rat?"

"With a super-rat. We have no choice."

Philip was right. SK540 alone stood there and sidled in as the door closed solidly again behind him.

How could one communicate with a rat? Philip could think of no way except to pick him up, place him where they were face to face, and talk.

"Are your—followers outside?" he asked.

A rodent's face can have no expression, but Philip caught a glance of contempt in the beady eyes. The slaves were doubtless bedded down in their hideaway, with strict orders to stay there and keep quiet.

"You know," Philip Vinson went on, "I could kill you, very easily." The words would mean nothing to SK540; the tone might. He watched the beady eyes; there was nothing in them but intelligent attention, no flicker of fear.

"Or I could tie you up and take you to the laboratory and let them decide whether to keep you or kill you. We are all much bigger and stronger than you. Without your army you can't intimidate us."

There was, of course, no answer. But SK540 did a startling and touching thing. He reached out one front paw, as if in appeal.

Norah caught her breath in astonishment.

•

"He—he just wants to be free," she said in a choked whisper.

"You mean you're not afraid of him any more?"

"You said yourself he couldn't intimidate us without his army."

Philip thought a minute. Then he said slowly:

"I wonder if we had the right to do this to him in the first place. He would have been an ordinary laboratory rat, mindless and contented; we've made him into a neurotic alien in his world."

"You're not responsible, darling; you're a technician, not a biochemist."

"I share the responsibility. We all do."

"So what? The fact remains that it was done, and here he is—and here we are."

The doorbell rang.

Philip and Norah exchanged glances. SK540 watched them.

"It's probably Kelly, from the lab," Philip said, "trying to find out why I wasn't there today. It's just about quitting time, and he lives nearest us."

Norah astonished him. She picked up SK540 from the bed-side table where Philip had placed him, and hid him under her pillow.

"Get rid of whoever it is," she said defensively. Philip stared for an instant, then walked briskly downstairs. He was back in a few minutes.

"It was Kelly, all right," he told her. "I said you were sick and I couldn't leave you to phone. I said I'd be there tomorrow. Now what?"

SK540's white whiskers emerged from under the pillow, and he jumped over to the table again. Norah's cheeks were pink.

"When it came to the point, I just couldn't," she explained shamefacedly. "I suddenly realized that he's a *person*. I couldn't let him be taken back to prison."

"Aren't you frightened any more?"

"Not of him." She faced the super-rat squarely. "Look," she said, "if we take care of you, will you get rid of that gang of yours, so we can be free too?"

"That's nonsense, Norah," Philip objected. "He can't possibly understand you."

"Dogs and cats learn to understand enough, and he's smarter than any dog or cat that ever lived."

"But—"

The words froze on his lips. SK540 had jumped to the floor and run to the door. There he stood and looked back at them, his tail twitching.

"He wants us to follow him," Norah murmured.

There was no sign of a hole in the back wall of the disused pantry. But behind it they could hear squeaks and rustlings.

SK540 scratched delicately at almost invisible cracks. A section of the wall, two by four inches, fell out on the floor.

"So that's where some of the oatmeal went," Norah commented. "Made into paste."

"Sh!"

SK540 vanished through the hole. They waited, listening to incomprehensible sounds. Outside it had grown dark.

•

Then the leader emerged and stood to one side of the long line that pattered through the hole. The two humans stared, fascinated, as the line made straight for the back door and under it. SK540 stayed where he was.

"Will they go back to the lab?" Norah asked.

Philip shrugged.

"It doesn't matter. Some of them may ... I feel like a traitor."

"I don't. I feel like one of those people who hid escaped war prisoners in Europe."

When the rats were all gone, they turned to SK540. But without a glance at them he re-entered the hiding-place. In a minute he returned, herding two white rats before him. He stood still, obviously expectant. Philip squatted on his heels. He picked up the two refugees and looked them over.

"Both females," he announced briefly. "And both pregnant."

"Is he the father?"

"Who else? He'd see to that."

"And will they inherit his—his—"

"His 'super-ratism'? That's the whole point. That's the object of the entire experiment. They were going to try it soon."

The three white rats had scarcely moved. The two mothers-to-be had apparently fallen asleep. Only SK540 stood quietly eying the humans.

When they left him to find a place where they could talk in private he did not follow them.

"It comes down to this," Philip said at the end of half an hour's fruitless discussion. "We promised him, or as good as. He believed us and trusted us.

"But if we keep to our promise we're *really* traitors—to the human race."

"You mean, if the offspring should inherit his brain-power, they might overrun us all?"

"Not might. Would."

"So—"

"So it's an insoluble problem, on our terms. We have to think of this as a war, and of them as our enemies. What is our word of honor to a rat?"

"But to a super-rat—to SK540—"

As if called, SK540 appeared.

Had he been listening? Had he understood? Neither of them dared to voice the question aloud in his presence.

"Later," Philip murmured.

"We must eat," said Norah. "Let's see what's left in the way of food."

•

Everything tasted flat; they weren't very hungry after all. There was enough left over to feed the three rats. But they had evidently helped themselves earlier; they left the scraps untasted.

Neither of the humans guessed what else had vanished from the pantry shelves—what, when he had heard enough, SK540 had slipped away and sprinkled on the remaining contents of the icebox, wherever the white powder would not show.

They did not know until it was too late—until both of them lay writhing in their last spasms on their bedroom floor.

By the time the house was broken into and their bodies found, SK540 and his two wives were far away, and safe....

And this, children, is the true account, handed down by tradition from the days of our great Founder, of how the human race ceased to exist and we took over the world.

One Way

I thought of every way to save Hal from the Lydna Project and failed ... but the women didn't!

We had the driver let us off in the central district and took a copter-taxi back to Homefield. There's no disgrace about it, of course; we just didn't feel like having all the neighbors see the big skycar with Lydna Project painted on its side, and then having them drop in casually to express what they would call interest and we would know to be curiosity.

There are people who boast that their sons and daughters have been picked for Lydna. What is there to boast about? It's pure chance, within limits.

And Hal is our only child and we love him.

Lucy didn't say a word all the way back from saying good-by to him. Lucy and I have been married now for 27 years and I guess I know her about as well as anybody on Earth does. People who don't know her so well think she's cold. But I knew what feelings she was crushing down inside her.

Besides, I wasn't feeling much like talking myself. I was remembering too many things:

Hal at about two, looking up at me—when I would come home dead-tired from a hard day of being chewed at by half a dozen bosses right up to the editor-in-chief whenever anything went the least bit out of kilter—with a smile that made all my tiredness disappear. Hal, when I'd pick him up at school, proudly displaying a Cybernetics Approval Slip (and ignoring the fact that half the other kids had one, too). Hal the day I took him to the Beard Removal Center, certain that he was a man, now that he was old enough for depilation. Hal that morning two weeks ago, setting out to get his Vocational Assignment Certificate....

That's when I stopped remembering.

It had been five years after our marriage before they let us start a child: some question about Lucy's uncle and my grandmother. Most parents aren't as old as we are when they get the news and usually have other children left, so it isn't so bad.

•

When we got home, Lucy still was silent. She took off her scarf and cloak and put them away, and then she pushed the button for dinner without even asking me what I wanted. I noticed, though, that she was ordering all the things I like. We both had the day off, of course, to go and say good-by to Hal—Lucy is a technician at Hydroponics Center.

I felt awkward and clumsy. Her ways are so different from mine; I explode and then it's over—just a sore place where it hurts if I touch it. Lucy never explodes, but I knew the sore place would be there forever, and getting worse instead of better.

We ate dinner in silence, though neither of us felt hungry, and had the table cleared. Then it was nearly 19 o'clock and I had to speak.

"The takeoff will be at 19:10," I said. "Want me to tune in now? Last year, when Mutro was Solar President, he gave a good speech before the kids left."

"Don't turn it on at all!" she said sharply. Then, in a softer voice, she added: "Of course, Frank, turn it on whenever you like. I'll just go to my room and open the soundproofing."

There were still no tears in her eyes.

I thought of a thousand things to say: Don't you want to catch a glimpse of Hal in the crowd going up the ramp? Mightn't they let the kids wave a last farewell to their folks listening and watching in? Mightn't something in the President's speech make us feel a little better?

But I heard myself saying, "Never mind, Lucy. Don't go. I'll leave the thing off."

I didn't want to be alone. I wanted Lucy there with me.

So we sat out the whole time of the visicast, side by side on the window-couch, holding hands. I'll say this for the neighbors—they must all have known, for Hal was the first to be selected from Homefield in nearly 40 years, and the newscast must have announced it over and over, but not a single person on the whole 62 floors of the house butted in on us. Not even that snoopy student from Venus in 47-14, who's always dropping in on other tenants and taking notes on "the mores of Earth Aboriginals." People can be very decent sometimes. We needn't have worried about coming home in the Lydna Project bus.

It was no good trying to keep my mind on anything else. Whether I wanted to or not, I had to relive the two last hours we'd ever have with Hal.

It couldn't mean to him what it meant to us. We were losing; he was both losing and gaining. We were losing our whole lives for 21 years past; he was, too, but he was entering a new life we would never know anything about. No word ever comes from Lydna; that's part of the project. Nobody even knows where it is for sure, though it's supposed to be one of the outer asteroids.

Both boys and girls are sent and there must be marriages and children—though probably the death-rate is pretty high, for every year they have to select 200 more from Earth to keep the population balanced. We would never know if our son married there, or whom, or when he died. We would never see our grandchildren, or even know if we had any.

•

Hal was a good son and I think we were fairly good parents and had made his childhood happy. But at 21, faced with a great, mysterious adventure and an unknown and exciting future, a boy can't be expected to be drowned in grief at saying good-by to his humdrum old father and mother. It might have been tougher for him 200 years ago, when they hadn't learned to decondition children early from parental fixations. But no youngster today would possess that kind of unwholesome dependency. If he did, he would never have been selected for Lydna in the first place.

That's one comfort we have—it's a sort of proof we had reared a child far above the average.

It was just weakness in me to half wish that Hal hadn't been so healthy, so handsome, so intelligent, so fine in character.

They were a wonderful lot. We said our good-bys in an enormous room of the spaceport, with this year's 200 selectees there from all over Earth, each with the relatives and whoever else had permission to make the last visit. I suppose it's a matter of accommodations and transportation, for nobody's allowed more than three. So it was mostly parents, with a few brothers, sisters and sweethearts or friends. The selectees themselves choose the names. After all, they've had two weeks after they were notified to say good-by to everyone else who matters to them.

Most of the time, all I could keep my mind on was Hal, trying to fix forever in my memory every last detail of him. We have dozens of sound stereos, of course, but this was the last time.

Still, it's my business at the News Office, and has been for 30 years, to observe people and form conclusions about them, so I couldn't help noticing with a professional eye some of the rest of the selectees. (This farewell visit is a private affair, and the press is barred, which is why I'd never been there before.)

There were two kinds of selectees that stood out, in my mind. One was those who had nobody at all to see them off. Completely alone, poor kids—orphans, doubtless, with no families and apparently not even friends near enough to matter. But, in a way, they would be the happiest; life on Earth couldn't have been very rewarding for them, and on Lydna they might find companionship. (If only companionship in misery, I thought—but I shied away from that. In our business, there are always leaks; we know—or guess—a few things about Lydna nobody else does, outside the authorities themselves. But we keep our mouths shut.)

The ones that tore my hearts were the boys and girls in love. They never take married people for Lydna, but a machine can't tell what a boy or girl is feeling about another girl or boy, and it's a machine that does the selecting. There's no use putting up an argument, for, once made, the choice is inexorable and unchangeable. In my work as a newsgatherer, I've heard some terrible stories. There have been suicide pacts and murders.

•

You could tell the couples in love. Not that there were any scenes. If there had been any in the two weeks past, they were over. But anybody who has learned to read human reactions, as I have, could recognize the agony those youngsters were going through.

I felt a deep gratitude that Hal wasn't one of them. He'd had his share of adolescent affairs, of course, but I was sure he was still just playing around. He'd seen a lot of Bet Milen, a girl a class ahead of him in school and college, but I didn't think she meant more to him than any of the others. If she had, she'd have been along to say good-by, but he'd asked for only the two of us. She was now a laboratory assistant in our hospital and could easily have gotten the time off.

It was growing late, almost midnight, and Lucy and I had to be at work tomorrow, no matter how we felt. I forced myself to talk, with Lucy's silent pain smothering me like a force-blanket. I made an effort and cleared my throat.

"Lucy, go to bed and turn on the hypno and try to get some sleep."

Lucy stood up obediently, but she shook her head. "You go, dear," she said, her voice firm. "I can't. I——"

The roof buzzer sounded. Somebody had landed in a copter and wanted us.

"Don't answer," I said quickly. "There's nobody we want to see——"

But she had already pushed the button to open the door.

It was Bet Milen, the girl Hal used to go around with.

I braced myself. This might be bad. She might have cared more for Hal than we had guessed.

But she didn't look grief-stricken. She looked excited, and determined, and a little bit frightened.

She scarcely glanced at me. She went right up to Lucy and took both Lucy's hands in hers.

"Well," she said in a clipped, tense voice, "we made it."
Then Lucy broke for the first time. The tears ran down her face and she didn't even wipe them away. "Are you *certain*?"

"Positive. And I got word to him. We'd agreed on a code. That's why he didn't want me there today—we couldn't trust ourselves not to betray it, either way."

I stood there staring at them, bewildered.

"What's this all about?" I demanded. "Have you two cooked up some crazy scheme to rescue Hal? I hope to heaven not! It would ruin all of us, including him!"

●

The wild daydreams I'd had myself flashed through my mind—the drug that would seem to kill him and wouldn't, the anonymous false accusation of subversion, the previous secret marriage. All impossible, all fatal.

Lucy disengaged her hands from the girl's and slipped her arm through mine.

"You tell him, Bet," she said gently. "You're the one who should."

I'd never noticed how pretty the girl was till then, when she stood there with her face flushed and her eyes straight on mine. A pang went through me; if only she and Hal could have—

"No, Mr. Sturt," she said, "we haven't rescued Hal. He's gone. But we've rescued part of him. I'm going to have his baby."

"Bet's going to live with us and be our daughter, Frank," Lucy explained. "Hal and she and I worked it out in these two weeks, after they came to me and told me how they felt about each other. We couldn't tell you till we were sure; I couldn't bear to have you hope and then be disappointed—it would be enough for me to have to suffer that."

"That is, I'll come if you want me here, Mr. Sturt," said Bet.

I had to sit down before I could speak. "Of course I want you. But what about your own family?"

"I haven't any. My mother's dead and my father's an engineer on Ganymede and gets home on leave about once in three years. I've been living in a youth hostel."

"But look here—" I turned to Lucy—"how on Earth can you know? Two weeks or less is no time—"

Lucy gave me a look I recognized, the patient one of the scientist for the layman.

"The Chow-Visalius test, dear. One day after the fertilized ovum starts dividing—"

"And I ran it myself every day for over a week. That's one of my jobs in the lab and it was easy to slip in another specimen. And it didn't, and it didn't and I went nearly out of my mind—"

"Every time Hal entered the apartment, I'd look at him and he'd shake his head," Lucy interrupted. "It meant everything to him. And it would just have broken my heart—"

"Mine, too," Bet said softly. "And his. And today was the last chance. I was scared to try it. This afternoon at 14:30, just before the farewell visits, was the deadline for viz messages to any of them. If I'd had to send mine without the word we'd agreed on that would tell him it was all right—But it was, at last! And now he knows, even if I never—even if we never—Excuse me, please, it's been a strain. I'm afraid I'm going to bawl."

·

We let her alone. Kids nowadays hate to be fussed over.

Us, we'd lost our son, and that was going to stay with us forever. But now we would have his child to love and—

An appalling thought struck me suddenly. I can't imagine why I hadn't realized it sooner. All this emotion, I suppose.

"Good God!" I cried. "An illegal child! We can't keep it!"

"Nobody's going to know," Lucy replied calmly. "Bet's going to live with us, and when it starts to show, she's going to take her allowed leave. We'll take ours, too, and we'll all go on a trip—to Mars, maybe, or Venus—one of the settled colonies where we can rent a house. Babies don't *have* to be born in hospitals, you know; our ancestors had them right at home. She's strong and healthy and I know what to do. Then we'll come back here and we'll have a baby with us that we adopted wherever we were. Nobody will ever know."

"Look," I said in a voice I tried to keep from rising. "There are four billion people on Earth and about 28 billion in the colonized Solar planets. Every one of those people is on record at Central Cybernetics. How do you suppose you're going to get away with the phony adoption of a non-existent child? The first time you have to take it to a baby clinic, they'll find it has no card."

"I thought of that," Lucy said, "and it can be done, because it must. Frank, for heaven's sake, use your wits! You're a newsgatherer. You know all sorts of people everywhere."

"I don't know any machines. And it's machines that handle the records."

"Machines under the supervision of humans."

"Sure," I said sarcastically. "I just go to my ex-newsgatherer pal who feeds the records to Io or Ceres and say, 'Look, old fellow, do me a favor, will you? My wife wants to adopt a baby from your colony, so just make up the names of two people and give them a life-check, invent their ancestors back to the time Central Cybernetics was established, and then slip in cards for their marriage, and the birth of their child—I'll let you know later whether to make it a boy or a girl—and then their deaths; and then my wife and I can adopt that made-up baby.'

"What kind of blackmailing hold do you think I have on any record official," I asked angrily, "to make him do a thing like that and keep his mouth shut about it? I could be eliminated for treason for even making such a suggestion."

"Frank, *think*! Surely there must be *some* way!"

•

And then it struck me. "Wait! I just got an idea. When I said 'treason,' just now—It might barely be possible—"

"Oh, what?"

"It would have to be Mars, the North Polar Cap colony. The K-Alph Conspiracy messed things up there badly."

"I remember, Mr. Sturt!" Bet said excitedly. "They wrecked everything in the three months before the rebellion was crushed, didn't they?"

"Everything including their cybernetics equipment. Central doesn't want it known, but I have inside information that it's still not in going condition. That colony is full of children who have never been registered. And I doubt if it will be in 100 per cent shape for the best part of another year. Those hellions really did a job. Let's see—this is the end of Month Two. We'd have to get away around Month Eight at the latest and the baby would be born—when exactly, Bet?"

"Early in Month Twelve. We could all be back here again by the first of next year, or even by the end of Month Thirteen."

"Well, I have enough accumulated leave for that and I guess you have too, Lucy; neither of us has taken more than two or three weeks for years. But what about you, Bet? You've been working less than a year."

"I can borrow it. Our director is crazy about travel and she'll be all for it when I tell her I have a chance to go to Mars for a long visit. Besides, she knows about Hal and me—I mean the way we are about each other—and she'll understand that I'd want to get away for a while now."

Asher, my editor-in-chief, would feel the same way, I thought, and so would Lucy's boss.

"I knew you'd find a way," remarked my wife complacently.

I looked at the telechron.

"We've all got to be at work in seven hours," I said, "if we expect to get through before the end of the afternoon. What say we turn in?"

"You stay here with us, Bet," said Lucy. "You parked your copter in our port, didn't you? Frank, I think we need a drink."

I pushed the buttons. Nobody said anything, but somehow it was a toast to Hal. I know the liquor had to get past a lump in my throat and the women were both crying. It wasn't like my self-contained Lucy. I guess she thought so herself, for she braced herself. But her voice was still trembling when she turned to Bet.

"A year from now," she said, "we'll all be back here in this room and, this time, part of Hal will be here with us—his son, our little Hal."

"It might be our little Hallie." Bet smiled through her tears. "It will be ten weeks before I can run the Schuster test to find out."

"It won't make any difference. Hal will never know that, but he'll know, way out there on Lydna, that his baby has been born. He'll know, even though he can never see it—or us."

•

Lucy blinked, then went on bravely. "Every time he looks in a mirror there, he'll say to himself, 'Well, back on Earth, there's a little tyke with my blue eyes and my curly hair and my mouth and nose and chin, who's going to grow up to be tall and straight like me—or maybe like Bet, but also a lot like me.'

"And as he grows older, he can think back to the way he was as a child and a boy and a man, and know that his son, or his daughter, will be feeling and thinking and looking some day just about the way he himself is then, and it will be a link with Earth and with us—"

That was when I had to go to the window and look out for a long time to pull myself together before I could face them again.

Lydna is top-top secret, but as I've said before, we newsgatherers get inside information.

I have a pretty shrewd idea of what the mysterious Lydna Project is. It's to alter human beings so they can adapt to the colonization of outer space.

The medics do things to them to enable them and their descendants to resist every possible condition of temperature and radiation and gravity. They have to alter the genes—acquired characters would be of use only in a short-term project, and this is long-term. But you can't alter genes without affecting the individual.

We'd have Hal's normal child.

But when Hal got to Lydna, he and the rest of them would be shocked and sick for a while at the sight of some of the inhabitants. And if he had any children on Lydna, we, back here, would scarcely recognize them as human. Some of them might have extra limbs. Some might have eyes and ears in odd places. Some might have lungs outside their bodies, or brains without a skull.

By that time, Hal himself would have got over being sick—unless, some time, he got hold of a mirror and remembered the boy he used to be.

The Margenes

There is a small striped smelt called the grunion which has odd egglaying habits. At high tide, on the second, third, and fourth nights after the full of the moon from March to June, thousands of female grunions ride in on the waves to a beach in southern California near San Diego, dig tail-first into the soft sand, deposit their eggs, then ride back on the wash of the next wave. The whole operation lasts about six seconds.

On the nights when the grunion are running, hordes of people used to come to the beach with baskets and other containers, and with torches to light the scene, and try to catch the elusive little fish in their hands. They were doing that on an April night in 1960. In the midst of the excitement of the chase, only a few of them noticed that something else was riding the waves in with the grunions.

Among the few who stopped grunion-catching long enough to investigate were a girl named Marge Hickin and a boy named Gene Towanda. They were UCLA students, "going together," who had come down on Saturday from Los Angeles for the fun.

"What on earth do you think these can be, Gene?" Marge asked, holding out on her palms three or four of the little circular, wriggling objects, looking like small-size doughnuts, pale straw in color.

"Never saw anything like them," Gene admitted. "But then my major's psychology, not zoology. They don't seem to bite, anyway. Here let's collect some of them instead of the fish. That dingus of yours will hold water. We can take them to the Marine Biology lab tomorrow and find out what they are."

Marge Hickin and Gene Towanda had started a world-wide economic revolution.

None of the scientists at the university laboratory knew what the little live straw-colored circles were, either. In fact, after a preliminary study they wouldn't say positively whether the creatures were animal or vegetable; they displayed voluntary movement, but they seemed to have no respiratory or digestive organs. They were completely anomalous.

The grunion ran again that night, and Gene and Marge stayed down to help the laboratory assistants gather several hundred of the strange new objects for further study. They were so numerous that they were swamping the fish, and the crowds at the beach began to grumble that their sport was being spoiled.

Next night the grunion stopped running—but the little doughnuts didn't. They never stopped. They came in by hundreds of thousands every night, and those which nobody gathered wriggled their way over the land until some of them even turned up on the highways (where a lot of them were smashed by automobiles), on the streets and sidewalks of La Jolla, and as far north as Oceanside and as far south as downtown San Diego itself.

The things were becoming a pest. There were indignant letters to the papers, and editorials were written calling on the authorities to do something. Just what to do, nobody knew; the only way to kill the circular little objects from the sea seemed to be to crush them—and they were too abundant for that to be very effective.

Meanwhile, the laboratory kept studying them.

Marge and Gene were interested enough to come down again the next weekend to find out what, if anything, had been discovered. Not much had: but one of the biochemists at the laboratory casually mentioned that chemically the straw-colored circles seemed to be almost pure protein, with some carbohydrates and fats, and that apparently they contained all the essential vitamins.

College student that he was, Gene Towanda immediately swallowed one of the wriggling things down whole, as a joke.

It tickled a little, but that wasn't what caused the delighted amazement on his face.

"Gosh!" he exclaimed. "It's delicious!"

He swallowed another handful.

That was the beginning of the great *margene* industry.

It was an astute reporter, getting a feature story on the sensational new food find, who gave the creatures their name, in honor of the boy and girl who had first brought the things to the attention of the scientists. He dubbed them margenes, and margenes they remained.

"Dr. O. Y. Willard, director of the laboratory," his story said in part, "thinks the margenes may be the answer to the increasing and alarming problem of malnutrition, especially in undeveloped countries.

"'For decades now,' he said, 'scientists have been worried by the growing gap between world population and world food facilities. Over-farming, climatic changes caused by erosion and deforestation, the encroachment of building areas on agricultural land, and above all the unrestricted growth of population, greatest in the very places where food is becoming scarcest and most expensive, have produced a situation where, if no remedy is found, starvation or semi-starvation may be the fate of half the Earth's people. The ultimate result would be the slow degeneration and death of the entire human race.

"'Many remedies have been suggested,' Dr. Willard commented further. 'They range from compulsory birth control to the production of synthetic food, hydroponics, and the harvesting of plankton from the oceans. Each of these presents almost insuperable difficulties.

"'The one ideal solution would be the discovery of some universal food that would be nourishing, very cheap, plentiful, tasty, and that would not violate the taboos of any people anywhere in the world. In the margenes we may have discovered that food.'

"'We don't know where the margenes came from,' the director went on to say, 'and we don't even know yet what they are, biologically speaking. What we do know is that they provide more energy per gram than any other edible product known to man, that everyone who has eaten them is enthusiastic about their taste, that they can be processed and distributed easily and cheaply, and that they are acceptable even to those who have religious or other objections to certain other foods, such as beef, among the Hindus or pork among the Jews and Mohammedans.

"'Even vegetarians can eat them,' Dr. Willard remarked, 'since they are decidedly not animal in nature. Neither, I may add, are they vegetable. They are a hitherto utterly unknown synthesis of chemical elements in living form. Their origin remains undiscovered.'"

Naturally, there was no thought of feeding people on raw margenes. Only a few isolated places in either hemisphere would have found live food agreeable. Experiment showed that the most satisfactory way to prepare them was to boil them alive, like crabs or lobsters. They could then be ground and pressed into cakes, cut into convenient portions. One one-inch-square cube made a nourishing and delicious meal for a sedentary adult, two for a man engaged in hard physical labor.

And they kept coming in from the Pacific Ocean nightly, by the million. By this time none of them had to be swept off streets or highways. The beach where for nearly a century throngs had gathered for the sport of catching grunion was off bounds now; it was the property of California Margene, Inc., a private corporation heavily subsidized by the Federal Government as an infant industry. The grunions themselves had to find another place to lay their eggs, or die off—nobody cared which. The sand they had used for countless millennia as an incubator was hemmed in by factory buildings and trampled by margene-gatherers. The whole beautiful shore for miles around was devastated; the university had to move its marine biological laboratory elsewhere; La Jolla, once a delightful suburb and tourist attraction, had become a dirty, noisy honkytonk town where processing and cannery workers lived and spent their off-hours; the unique Torrey Pines had been chopped down because they interfered with the erection of a freight airport.

But half the world's people were living on margenes.

The sole possession of this wonderful foodstuff gave more power to the United States than had priority in the atomic bomb. Only behind the Iron Curtain did the product of California Margene, Inc. fail to penetrate. *Pravda* ran parallel articles on the same day, one claiming that margenes—*brzdichnoya*—had first appeared long ago on a beach of the Caspian Sea and had for years formed most of the Russian diet; the other warning the deluded nations receiving free supplies as part of American foreign aid that the margenes had been injected with drugs aimed at making them weak and submissive to the exploitation of the capitalist-imperialists.

There was a dangerous moment at the beginning when the sudden sharp decline in stocks of all other food products threatened another 1929. But with federal aid a financial crash was averted and now a new high level of prosperity had been established. Technological unemployment was brief, and most of the displaced workers were soon retained for jobs in one of the many ramifications of the new margene industry.

Agriculture, of course, underwent a short deep depression, not only in America but all over the world; but it came to an end as food other than margenes quickly became a luxury product. Farmers were able to cut their production to a small fraction of the former yield, and to get rich on the dizzying prices offered for bread, apples, or potatoes. And this increased the prosperity of the baking and other related industries as well.

In fact, ordinary food costs (which meant margene costs) were so low that a number of the larger unions voluntarily asked for wage decreases in their next contracts. California Margene, Inc. was able to process, pack, and distribute margene cakes at an infinitesimal retail price, by reason of the magnitude of the output.

An era of political good feeling fell upon the western world, reflected from the well-fed comfort of vast populations whose members never before in their lives had had quite enough to eat. The fear of famine seemed to be over forever, and with it the fear of the diseases and the social unrest that follow famine. Even the U.S.S.R. and its satellites, in a conciliatory move in the United Nations Assembly, suggested that the long cold war ought to be amenable to a reasonable solution through a series of amicable discussions. The western nations, assenting, guessed shrewdly that the Iron Curtain countries "wanted in" on the margenes.

Marge Hickin and Gene Towanda, who had started it all, left college for copywriting jobs with the agency handling the enormous margene publicity; they were married a few months later.

And the margenes continued to come in from the sea in countless millions. They were being harvested now from the Pacific itself, near the shoreline, before they reached the beach. Still no research could discover their original source.

Only a few scientists worried about what would happen if the margenes should disappear as suddenly as they had arrived. Attempts at breeding the creatures had failed completely. They did not undergo fission, they did not sporulate, they seemed to have no sex. No methods of reproduction known in the plant or animal kingdom seemed to apply to them. Hundreds of them were kept alive for long periods—they lived with equal ease in either air or water, and they did not take nourishment, unless they absorbed it from their environment—but no sign of fertility ever appeared. Neither did they seem to die of natural causes. They just kept coming in....

On the night of May 7, 1969, not a single margene was visible in the ocean or on the beach.

They never came again.

What happened as a result is known to every student of history. The world-wide economic collapse, followed by the fall of the most stable governments, the huge riots that arose from the frantic attempts to get possession of the existing stocks of margene cakes or of the rare luxury items of other edibles, the announcement by the U.S.S.R. that it had known from the beginning the whole thing was a gigantic American hoax in the interests of the imperialistic bloodsuckers, the simultaneous atomic attacks by east and west, the Short War of 1970 that ruined most of what bombs had spared of the Earth, the slow struggle back of the remnant of civilization which is all of existence you and I have ever known—all these were a direct outgrowth of that first appearance of the margenes on the beach near San Diego on an April night in 1960.

Marge and Gene Towanda were divorced soon after they had both lost their jobs. She was killed in the hydrogen blast that wiped out San Diego; he fell in the War of 1970. "Margene" became a dirty word in every language on Earth. What small amount of money and ability can be spared is, as everyone knows, devoted today to a desperate international effort to reach and colonize another habitable planet of the Solar System, if such there be.

.

As for the margenes, themselves, out of the untold millions that had come, only a few thousand were lucky enough to survive and find their way back to their overcrowded starting-point. In their strange way of communication—as incomprehensible to us as would be their means of nourishment and reproduction, or their constitution itself—they made known to their kin what had happened to them. There is no possibility, in spite of the terrific over-population of their original home and of the others to which they are constantly migrating, that they will ever come here again.

There has been much speculation, particularly among writers of science fiction, on what would happen if aliens from other planets should invade Earth. Would they arrive as benefactors or as conquerors? Would we welcome them or would we overcome and capture them and put them in zoos and museums? Would we meet them in friendship or with hostility?

The margenes gave us the answer.

Beings from outer space came to Earth in 1960.

And we ate them.

The Akkra Case

Deliberate murder being so very rare a crime in our society, an account of any instance of it must attract the attention not only of criminologists but also of the general public. Very many of my auditors must remember the Akkra case well, since it occurred only last year. This, however, is the first attempt to set forth the bizarre circumstances hitherto known only to the authorities and to a few specialists.

On February 30 last, the body of a young girl was found under the Central Park mobilway in Newyork I. She had been struck on the head with some heavy object which had fractured her skull, and her auburn hair was matted with congealed blood. Two boys illegally trespassing on one of the old dirt roads in the park itself stumbled upon the corpse. She was fully dressed, but barefoot, with her socsandals lying beside her. An autopsy showed only one unusual thing—she was a virgin, though she was fully mature.

Two hundred years ago, say, this would have been a case for the homicide branch of the city police. Now, of course, there are no city police, all local law enforcement being in the hands of the Federal government, with higher supervision and appeal to the Interpol; and since there has been no reported murder (except in Africa and China, where this crime has not yet been entirely eradicated) for at least 20 years, Fedpol naturally has no specialists in homicide. Investigation therefore was up to the General Branch in Newyork Complex I.

The murderer had stupidly broken off the welded serial number disc from her wristlet—stupidly, because of course everybody's fingerprints and retinal pattern are on file with Interpol from birth. It was soon discovered that the victim was one Madolin Akkra, born in Newyork I of mixed Irish, Siamese, and Swedish descent, aged 18 years and seven months. Since it is against the law for any minor (under 25) to be gainfully employed, and there was no record of any exemption-permit, she had necessarily to be a student. She was found to be studying spaceship maintenance at Upper Newyork Combined Technicum.

People who deride Fedpol and call it a useless anachronism don't know what they are talking about. It is true that in our society criminal tendencies are understood to be a disease, amenable to treatment, not a free-will demonstration of anti-social proclivities. But it is also true that every member of Fedpol, down to the merest rookie policeman, is a trained specialist in some field, and that most of its officers are graduate psychiatrists. As soon as Madolin Akkra's identity was determined, it was easy to find out everything about her.

•

The circumstances surrounding her in life were sufficiently odd in themselves. Her mother was dead, but she lived with her own father and full younger sister in a small (only 20 stories and 80 living-units) co-operative apartment house in the old district formerly called Westchester, once an "exclusive" settlement but now considerably run down, and populated for the most part by low-income families. Few of the residents had more than one helicopter per family, and many of them had to commute to their jobs or schools by public copter. The building where the Akkras lived was shabby, its chrome and plastic well worn, and showed the effects of a negligent local upkeep system. The Akkras even prepared and ate some of their meals in their own quarters—an almost unheard-of anachronism.

The father had served his 20 years of productive labor from 25 to 45, and the whole family was therefore supported by public funds of one sort or another. When the Fedpol officers commenced their investigation by interviewing this man, they found him one of the worst social throwbacks discovered in many years—doubtless a prime reason for the bizarre misfortune which had overtaken his misguided daughter. To begin with, the investigators wanted to know, why had he not reported his daughter missing? To this, Pol Akkra made the astonishing reply that the girl was old enough to know her own business, and that he had never asked any questions as to what she did! Everyone knows it is every adult's responsibility to report any deviation by the young more serious than the mischievous trespassing by the boys who had found Madolin Akkra's body, and who at least had gone to Fedpol at once. The officers could get no lead whatever from the girl's father.

To find the murderer, it was of first importance to establish the background of this strange case. Access to the park is difficult—has been difficult ever since, more than a century ago, the area became a hunting-ground for thieves and hoodlums, and was transformed into a cultivated forest and garden preserved for aesthetic reasons, and to be viewed only from the mobilways above. (The boys who found the body are, of course, proof that the sealing-off of the park is not entirely effective—but surely only a daring and agile child could insinuate himself under the thorn-set hedges surrounding the park, or swing down to the tree-tops from the structure above.)

If the victim had been killed elsewhere, how was her body carried to the spot where it was found? Both murderer and corpse would have had to penetrate unobserved into an almost impenetrable area. Could the body have been thrown from above? But if so, how could the remains of a full-grown girl have been transported from either a ground car or a copter on to the crowded mobilway, brightly lighted all night long? She must have gone there alive, either under duress or of her own accord.

The first and most natural question, to Fedpol, was: who did have access to the park? The answer was, the gardeners. But the gardeners were out: they were all robots, even their supervisor. No robot is able to harm a human being. Moreover, no robot could have brought the victim in from outside if she had been killed elsewhere. The gardeners never leave the park, and they would repel any strange robot from elsewhere who tried to enter it. And one could hardly imagine a sane human being who would go to the park for a rendezvous with a robot!

•

It was Madolin's little sister, Margret, who interrupted the futile interrogation of the surly and resistant Pol Akkra and provided the first clue. She caught the eye of the investigating officer, Inspector Dugal Kazazian, and quietly went into the next room, where Kazazian followed her after posting his assistant with the father.

"I promised Madolin I would never tell on her," she whispered, "but now she's—now it doesn't matter." She had loved her sister; her eyes were puffy from weeping. "She—she'd been going to Naturist get-togethers."

Kazazian almost groaned aloud. He might have known—this was the first time they had been linked with murder, but it seemed to him that in almost every other affair he had investigated for the past few years, the subversive Naturists somehow had crept in. And if he had reflected, he would have suspected them already, since there seems to be no school or college which does not harbor an underground branch of these criminal lunatics.

I need hardly explain to my auditors who and what the Naturists are. But to keep the record complete, let me say briefly that this pernicious worldwide conspiracy, founded 50 years ago by the notorious Ali Chaim

Pertinuzzi, is engaged in an organized campaign to tear down all the marvelous technical achievements of our civilization. It pretends to believe that we should eat "natural" foods and wear "natural" textiles instead of synthetics, walk instead of ride, teach children the obsolete art of reading (reading what?—the antique books preserved in museums?), make our own music, painting, and sculpture instead of enjoying the exquisite products of perfected machines, open up all parks and the few remaining rural preserves to campers, hunters and fishers (if any specimens worth hunting can be found outside zoos), and what they call "hikers"—in a word, go back to the confused, reactionary world of our ancestors. From this hodgepodge of "principles" it is a natural transition to political and economic subversion. No wonder that the information that Madolin Akkra had been corrupted by this vile outfit sent a chill down Inspector Kazazian's spine.

•

It explained a great deal, however. The Naturists profess to oppose our healthy system of sexual experimentation, and Madolin had been a virgin. The weird family situation, and her father's attitude both toward her and toward the Fedpol, aroused suspicion that he too was affiliated with the Naturists, not simply that Madolin had flirted with the outer edges of the treasonable organization, as a "fellow-seeker," without her father's knowledge.

Suppose the girl, fundamentally decent and ethically-minded, had revolted against the false doctrine and threatened to betray its advocates? Then she might have been killed to silence her—and what more likely than that, as a piece of brazen defiance, her murdered corpse should have been deposited in the only bit of "natural" ground still remaining in the Newyork area?

But how, and by whom?

•

The first step, of course, was to fling a dragnet around all known or suspected Naturists in the district. In a series of flying raids they were rounded up; and since there no longer exist those depositories for offenders formerly known as prisons, they were kept incommunicado in the psychiatric wards of the various hospitals. For good measure, Pol Akkra was included. Margret, at 13, was old enough to take care of herself.

Next, all Madolin's classmates at the Technicum, the operators of her teach-communicators, and members of other classes with whom it was learned she had been on familiar terms, were subjected to an intensive electronic questioning. (Several of these were themselves discovered to be tainted with Naturism, and were interned with the rest.) One of the tenets of Naturism is a return to the outworn system of monogamy, and the questioning was directed particularly to the possibility that Madolin had formed half of one of the notorious Naturist "steady couples," who often associate without or before actual mating. But day after day the investigators came up with not the slightest usable lead.

Please do not think I am underrating Fedpol. Nothing could have been more thorough than the investigation they undertook. But this turned out in the end to be a case which by its very nature obfuscated the normal methods of criminological science. Fedpol itself has acknowledged this, by its formation in recent months of the Affiliated Assistance Corps, made up of amateurs who volunteer for the detection of what are now called Class X crimes—those so far off the beaten path that professionals are helpless before them.

For it was an amateur who solved Madolin Akkra's murder—her own little sister. When Margret Akkra reaches the working age of 25 she will be offered a paid post as Newyork Area Co-ordinator of the AAC.

•

Left alone by her father's internment, Margret began to devote her whole time out of school hours to the pursuit of the person or persons who had killed her sister. She had told Kazazian all she actually knew; but that was only her starting-point. Though she herself, as she had told the Inspector, believed that the murder might be traced to Madolin's connection with the Naturist (and though she probably at least suspected her father to be involved with them also), she did not confine herself to that theory, as the Fedpol, with its scientific training, was obliged to do. Concealed under a false floor in her father's bedroom—mute evidence of his Naturist affiliation—she found a cache of printed books—heirlooms which should long ago have been presented to a museum for consultation by scholars only. They dated back to the 20th century, and were of the variety then known as "mystery stories." Margret of course could not read them. But she remembered now, with revulsion, how, when she and Madolin were small children, their mother had sometimes (with windows closed and the videophone turned off) amused them by telling them ancient myths and legends that by their very nature Margret now realized must have come from these contraband books.

Unlike her father and her sister, and apparently her mother as well, Margret Akkra had remained a wholesome product of a civilized education. She had nothing but horror and contempt for the subversive activities in the midst of which, she knew now, she had grown up. The very fact, which became plain to her for the first time, that her parents had lived together, without changing partners, until her mother had died, was evidence enough of their aberration.

But, stricken to the heart as the poor girl was, she could not cease to love those she had always loved, or to be diverted from her resolution to solve her sister's murder. Shudder as she might at the memory of those subversive books, she yet felt they might inadvertently serve to assist her.

It was easy to persuade the school authorities that her shock and distress over Madolin's death had slowed up her conscious mind, and to get herself assigned to a few sessions with the electronic memory stimulator. It took only two or three to bring back in detail the suppressed memories, and to enable her to extrapolate from them.

•

One feature of these so-called "mysteries" that came back to her struck Margret with especial force—the frequent assertion that murderers always return to the scene of their crime. She decided that she too must plant herself at the spot where her sister's body had been found, and lie in wait for the returning killer.

It would be useless to try to obtain official permission, but she was only 13, as lean and agile as any other child, and if boys could evade the hedges and the robot gardeners, so could she. The audiovids had displayed plenty of pictures of the exact scene, and Margret knew where to find it. But an inspection of the hedges showed her that it would be easier for her to get in from above, at night—a likelier time also for her prey.

She located a place where the trees grew almost to the mobilway and shaded a section of it between the lamps. Perched on the stand-pave and watching for a pause in the stream of gliders-by, she dropped lightly into a tree and climbed down to the park beneath. Hiding from the gardeners, she made her way to the bushes where the boys had discovered Madolin. For nearly a week, fortified by Sleepnomer pills, Margret spent every moment after dark in this hideaway. It was a long, nerve-wracking vigil: the close contact with leaves and grass, the sound of the wind in the trees, the unaccustomed darkness away from the lights above, the frightening approach of wild squirrels and rabbits and even birds, the necessity to stay concealed from passing robots, kept her on edge. But stubbornly she persisted. And at last she was rewarded.

It was not late—only about 20 o'clock—when she heard a scramble and bump not far from her own means of access to the park. It was not the first time since her watch began that she had heard other adventurers, invariably small and rather scared boys who dared one another to walk for a few feet along the dirt paths, then in a panic rushed back the way they had come. But this time the steps came directly toward her—human footsteps, not the shuffle of a robot.

Hidden behind a bush, Margret saw them approach—two boys of about her own age. And then, with a sickening lurch of her heart, she recognized them. She had seen them, acclaimed as heroes, on the videoscreen. They were the two who had found Madolin. She could hear every word they said.

"Come on," one of them urged in a hoarse whisper. "There's nothing to be afraid of."

"Yes, there is," the other objected. "Ever since then, they've got the gardeners wired to describe and report anybody they find inside the park."

"I don't care. We've *got* to find it. Give me the beamer."

•

Margret crouched behind the thickest part of the shrubbery, her infra-red camera at the alert. The tape-attachment was already activated.

The second boy still held back. "I told you then," he muttered, "that we shouldn't have reported it at all. We should have got out of here and never said a word to anyone."

"We couldn't," the first boy said, shocked. "It would have been anti-social. Haven't you ever learned anything in school?"

"Well, it's anti-social to kill somebody, too, isn't it?"

Margret pressed the button on the camera. Enlarged enough, even the identification discs on the boys' wristlets would show.

"How could we guess there was a human being there, except us? What was she doing here, anyway? Come on, Harri, we've got to find that thing. It's taken us long enough to get a chance to sneak in here."

"Maybe they've found it already," said Harri fearfully.

"No, they haven't; if they had, they'd have taken us in as soon as they dusted the fingerprints."

"All right, it's not anywhere on the path. Put the beamer on the ground where it will shine in front of us, and let's get down on our stomachs and hunt underneath the bushes."

Grabbing her camera, Margret jumped to her feet and dashed past the startled boys. She heard a scream—that would be Harri—and then their feet pounding after her. But she had a head start, and her eyes were more accustomed to the dark than theirs could be. She reached a tree, shinnied up it, jumped from one of its limbs to another on a higher tree beneath the mobilway, chinned herself up, and made her way out safely.

She went straight to Fedpol headquarters and asked for Inspector Kazazian.

The frightened boys were picked up at once. They were brought into headquarters, where they had been praised and thanked before, and as soon as they saw the pictures and heard the tape-recording they confessed everything.

That night, they said, they were being initiated into one of those atavistic fraternities which it seems impossible for the young to outgrow or the authorities to suppress. As part of their ordeal, they had been required to sneak into Central Park and to bring back as proof of their success a captured robot gardener. Between them they had decided that the only way they could ever get their booty would be to disassemble the robot, for though it could not injure them, if they took hold of it, its communication-valve would blow and the noise would bring others immediately; so they had taken along what seemed to them a practical weapon—a glass brick pried out of the back of a locker in the school gym. Hurled by a strong and practiced young arm, it could de-activate the robot's headpiece.

When, as they waited in the darkness for a gardener to appear, they saw a figure moving about in the shrubbery bordering the path, one of them—neither would say which one it was—let fly. To their horror, instead of the clang of heavy glass against metal, they heard a muffled thud as the brick struck flesh and bone. They started to run away. But after a few paces they forced themselves to return.

It was a girl, and the blow had knocked her flat. Her head was bleeding badly and she was moaning. Terrified, they knelt beside her. She gasped once and lay still. One of the boys laid a trembling hand on her breast, the other seized her wrist. There was no heart-beat and there was no pulse. On an impulse, the boy holding her wrist wrenched away her identification disc.

Panic seized them, and they dashed away, utterly forgetting the brick, which at their first discovery one of them had had the foresight to kick farther into the shrubbery, out of view. Sick and shaking, they made their way out of the park and separated. The boy who had the disc threw it into the nearest sewer-grating.

The next day, after school, they met again and talked it over. Finally they decided they must go to Fedpol and report; but to protect themselves they would say only that they had found a dead body.

•

Day after day, they kept seeing and hearing about the case on the videaud, and pledged each other to silence. Then suddenly one of the boys had a horrible thought—they had forgotten that the brick would show their fingerprints!... They had come desperately to search for it when Margret overheard them. Kazazian's men found it without any difficulty; it had been just out of the gardeners' regular track.

In view of the accidental nature of the whole affair, and the boys' full confession, they got off easy. They were sentenced to only five years' confinement in a psychiatric retraining school.

The suspects against whom nothing could be proved were released and kept under surveillance. Pol Akkra, and all the proved Naturists, were sentenced to prefrontal lobotomies. Margret Akkra, in return for her help in solving the mystery, secured permission to take her father home with her. A purged and docile man, he was quite capable of the routine duties of housekeeping.

The killing of Madolin Akkra was solved. But one question remained: how and why had she been in Central Park at all?

The answer, when it came, was surprising and embarrassingly simple. And this is the part that has never been told before.

Pol Akkra, a mere simulacrum of the man he had been, no longer knew his living daughter or remembered his dead one. But in the recesses of his invaded brain some faint vestiges of the past lingered, and occasionally and unexpectedly swam up to his dreamlike consciousness.

One day he said suddenly: "Didn't I once know a girl named Madolin?"

"Yes, father," Margret answered gently, tears in her eyes.

"Funny about her." He laughed his ghastly Zombie chuckle. "I *told* her that was a foolish idea, even if it was good Nat—Nat-something theory."

"What idea was that?"

"I—I've forgotten," he said vaguely. Then he brightened. "Oh, yes, I remember. Stand barefoot in fresh soil for an hour in the light of the full moon and you'll never catch cold again.

"She was subject to colds, I think." (About the only disease left we have as yet no cure for.) He sighed. "I wonder if she ever tried it."

Time Out for Redheads

His name was Mikel Skot. He was thirty-four, five-feet-ten and lean, with decent features and all his hair and quite nice brown eyes. But somehow he always seemed to give the impression of being of indeterminate age, and slightly dusty. He lived alone, he gravitated between his job and his lodgings, and since the age of fourteen he had never known a girl well enough to call her by her first name.

For twelve years, ever since 2827, he had sold tickets at one of the windows of Time Travel Tours, Unlimited. If raises hadn't been automatic, he would never have had one, though he was punctual, faithful, honest, quick and accurate. Even the other ticket-sellers still called him Citizen Skot.

He had never budged from his cozy era—even though, as an employee, he was entitled to take any tour he wished, on his semi-annual vacation, at no cost to him beyond the planetary sales tax—nor had he ever left his native city, let alone his native planet. He was too shy even to realize he was lonely.

This morning there was the usual rush. Staggered vacations meant that any time of the year was the busy season for TTT. Skillfully Mikel Skot arranged tours and calculated rates.

"Two weeks in Rome, 45 B.C.? That will be creds 850, Citizen. You get your costume and equipment in Room 104, right off the Teleport. Yes, I'm sure they'll have a Latin language-transformer you can hire." "England in 1600, one month, reservation in the name of Chas Rusl. Yes, I have it right here. That will be creds 500, please." "You mean you want a ticket for here in Los, for a week six years ago in February? Why, yes, it's a little unusual, but—oh, certainly, I understand—a second honeymoon. Congrats, Citizen—not many couples stay together that long! Just a min, while I look up the rate for two."

The queue seemed endless, and crowds of travelers who already had their tickets were pushing their way through the doors back of the ticket-office to the Teleport itself, together with the friends who were seeing them off. If Mikel had had a moment to spare, which he hadn't, he might have wondered, as so often before, at the numbers of people everybody except himself seemed to know.

The morning wore on, and he was beginning to think longingly of 13:30 o'clock, when his lunchtime relief would arrive and he could sit in a quiet corner of an Autocaf and watch the tridimens screen for the day's news while he ate his favorite vitatabs and smoked a healthcig.

Then everything happened all at once.

The girl standing at his ticket-window was a redhead. Her eyes were green, with little dancing amber lights in them, and she smiled at him as if he were the kind of man girls do smile at, and not ineffectual Mikel Skot.

"Can you tell me," she began, in a warm, slightly husky voice.

Then she screamed loudly and collapsed.

•

There were shouts and jostling and milling around, and somebody leaned over the counter and abruptly thrust something into his hand. He stood there dazed, grabbing the object, whatever it was. Then he leaned over the counter. The girl was lying there, very still. On one side of her a pool of blood was slowly forming on the floor.

The guards were coming from all directions, trying to get some kind of quiet and order into the excited throng. Mikel looked down at the thing in his hand.

It was a knife, a steel knife with a wooden handle. It was obviously an antique, and of great value. And it was smeared with fresh blood.

Mikel Skot lost his head entirely. Never before had he, or anyone he had ever heard of, been involved even remotely in any kind of violence. He never even took in historical crime plays. The redheaded girl was dead, and he held in his hand the knife that had killed her. And she had been the first girl who had smiled at him for years.

He wanted out—now!

He reached behind him and grabbed a ticket at random, not even looking to see what date it was. He punched it hastily for a week.

Nobody was looking at him; everybody was still yelling at everybody else, and the sweating guards were trying to line people up and blocking the doors so that they could not get away. Mikel ran to the corridor in back of the counters, which the ticket-sellers used, and saw that the company door to the Teleport was open. Out there, what with parties singing "Happy Timetrav to You," or noisily greeting homecomers, and the loudspeaker directing passengers to their proper stations, and the roar of the take-offs and returnjets, nobody seemed to have noticed that anything was wrong in the ticket-office.

Mikel glanced around once to be sure that nobody was watching him, and slipped through the door. He was still holding the knife. Automatically he thrust it into his belt-pouch.

It was typical of him that after twelve years not one of the Teleport attendants knew him by sight. He thrust his ticket at the nearest one. The man glanced at it (three other travelers were trying to get his attention at the same time) and said "Platform Eight." Mikel hurried there.

Before he reached it he remembered something. He had punched the ticket for duration, but not for place. Well, that was all right. If it had no place-punch, it would mean Los itself. He was escaping into his own city.

The attendant at Eight took his ticket, then peered at him dubiously.

"You haven't clothes for the period, Citizen. Go to Room 104 and—"

"It doesn't matter," Mikel interrupted him. He was in a fever to be gone. "I'm—it's a research project," he added in a sudden inspiration which didn't make sense even to himself, but which the attendant, used to strange statements from travelers, accepted without comment. He sealed the timeporter on to Mikel's wrist, set it for return in a week, and helped him into the telechamber.

There was a swift moment when his head felt empty and his stomach heaved: and Mikel Skot found himself sitting on an iron bench in a park. He had a week now to think things over. He was in Los—he had to be, his ticket said so.

But when?

He looked about him. It must be the middle of the day, the same time it had been before, and the park was full of people on their lunch-hour. They were dressed weirdly—the men and half the women wore tight cylindrical garments, one on each leg. The upper part of their bodies were covered with various kinds of brightly-colored cloth, though occasionally he saw a woman who wore only a breast-holder above her bare midriff! Mikel, in his belted tunic, huddled in a corner of his bench, fearful of notice. But nobody paid any attention to him, and once a man passed who had on a tunic too—a long white one, over bare feet and under long hair and a flowing beard. Apparently in this period people dressed as they pleased—at least in Los.

The city itself, what part of it he could see from his vantage-point, was stranger than the people. There were no moving sidewalks, and no weather-canopies over the streets—though perhaps these had only been removed for the dry season. The buildings looked shrunken and tiny—hardly one seemed to be more than thirty or forty stories high. Archaic buses and motor-cars, apparently powered by some non-atomic fuel, plied the actual streets, instead of being confined to subways. The skies were almost empty of planes, and those he saw were incredibly clumsy and slow. There was obviously no freeway for helicopters.

•

It was self-evident that he was in some year of the remote past, though just which, he had no idea. He wished he had taken time to glance at the ticket before he handed it in. He wished he had studied history komikbooks, or given more than a cursory glance at the telescreen propinforms of TTT. There was something to be said, after all, for the General Educationalists, cranks as they were.

Certainly this was not his Los—his giant city stretching from Mex to Sanfran without a break. This was a little place of probably not much more than two million inhabitants. Well, here he was for a week, and he'd better find out how he was going to eat and sleep. Properly equipped time travelers had money of the right period, but the cred checks in his pouch would do him no good now. What did he have on him that could be exchanged for board and lodging?

Only one object of undoubted value. The knife.

Surreptitiously and with distaste he took it out and looked at it. The blood had dried on it and doubtless left traces on the lining of his pouch. It was probably covered with the fingerprints of the murderer as well as with his own. But it was all he had.

In the middle of the park there was a fountain, with a pool around it. Casually Mikel Skot strolled over to it and sat down on the ledge. When he was sure nobody was looking he dipped the knife in the water and scrubbed it dry on the inner hem of his tunic. There would still be traces of blood which any chemist could find, of course; but nobody here would be examining it for that. Since anyone could see that it was of immense value, he would have to account for possession of it. He could say it was an heirloom.

Putting it back in his pouch he approached a fat man on a bench nearby.

"Where is the nearest history museum, please, Citizen?" he asked politely.

The man looked up. He had been scanning a large piece of paper which Mikel, with a thrill, recognized from one of his few visits to the Museum of Antiquities. It was a thing called a newspaper, which had antedated the tridimens telescreen. He remembered that the specimens he had seen had borne dates at the top, and if he could read the archaic printing he could find out what year it was. But the man folded it up and thrust it under his arms as he answered.

"History museum?" he echoed. "Gosh, bud, I don't know. I'm a stranger here myself—just got in from Kansas yesterday. You a foreigner?" he asked with frank curiosity. "You got a funny accent. And you sure look funny."

A foreigner—that was a good one! But Mikel had no time to waste. He murmured "Excuse," and left. The man stared after him and made a gesture which Mikel did not understand—describing a circle in the air near his forehead.

Mikel walked to the edge of the little park and looked about him. Across the street was a store with newspapers in racks in front of it. He could go over there and see the dates. But what did it really matter? With his ignorance of all but the haziest generalities of history—he thought that once, thousands of years ago, Los had belonged to the Spaniards, and after that there was some kind of war that was maybe called the American Revolution or the Civil War or the World War, he was not sure which—it wouldn't do him much good to know whether he was in, say, 1820 or 1960 or 2080. Besides, he was afraid to cross that street full of clumsy vehicles, and with neither an overpass nor an underpass. Nowhere could he see anything that resembled a museum.

•

Farther down on the same side of the street on which he stood, he saw something that looked faintly promising. He walked down to it, and found a window full of odd-looking primitive objects, the nature of some of which he could not guess. But there were knives among them, and a sign said, in ancient spelling, "Jewelry Bought and Sold." On an impulse he walked in.

A man in another queer garment—some kind of cloth upper, with a white linen thing beneath it and a ribbon tied around his neck—looked up without surprise at Mikel's literally untimely garb, and said: "Yes, sir?"

Mikel drew out the knife.

"Very valuable," he said. "An heirloom. How much will you give me?"

The man shrank back, not as if he were afraid of the knife, but as if he were suddenly afraid of Mikel.

"You kidding me?" he asked. "Or is this a stick-up?"

Mikel was not sure what the words meant, so he merely shook his head.

"Then are you nuts? There's nothing valuable about that thing. It's just an ordinary kitchen knife."

"Not valuable?" Mikel's face fell. "But look—wooden handle, steel blade."

"So what? Every knife has a wooden handle and a steel blade."

"You will not give me money for it?"

"Of course not. We don't buy junk."

There was no use arguing. One age's antique is another age's junk. Mikel sighed and departed quietly. How was he to get food and shelter for a week?

He went back to the park and sat down again on a bench. He put the knife back in his pouch.

This was what came of panicking for the first time in his humdrum life. A sudden image of the redheaded girl came before his mind—her green eyes and her smile. That girl—she was so pretty—and she had smiled at him, whom girls never noticed. And then she had been killed. Now that it was too late, he wished he had stayed, whatever might have happened to him. He wanted to help, to avenge her; he wanted to be home again. His stomach reminded him sharply that he had had no lunch. He had never heard how long a man could go without eating. Could he even live through the week?

He sat there disconsolately, his eyes fixed on the ground. On his wrist was sealed the little gadget that was his only means of ever seeing 2839 again.

Somebody came and sat down beside him. Deep in thought, he did not even glance up. A voice said, "Can you tell me what time it is? My watch is broken and there's no clock around here."

"Watch"—that meant "to be alert." "Clock"—that was an ancient time-measuring device, he thought. The only way Mikel knew to tell the time was to glance at the ceiling of any room, or if he were outdoors to tune in on his miniature tridimens gadget, attached to his belt. He dialed it now, but there was no response. Of course not—it wouldn't work across perhaps a thousand years.

"I'm sorry," he answered. "I can't."

He turned as he spoke. He jumped violently.

The speaker was a girl. She had red hair and green eyes. Otherwise there was no resemblance, though she too was pretty. But red hair and green eyes seemed to be haunting him.

"What's that thing on your left wrist, then?" asked the girl spunkily.

•

Mikel reddened. Rule Five of the booklets he handed out with the tickets to all travelers leaped into his mind: "Remember, you cannot change the course of history. To avoid confusion and difficulty, avoid revealing to any person you meet in other time-periods the true nature of your presence there."

He broke the rule, and was sorry at once.

"It's a timeporter," he said, "set for my return home."

The girl laughed.

"That's a good one. I thought I'd heard everything since I came to this crazy place. What are you, an Arab, dressed in that tablecloth?"

"I was born right here in Los," Mikel announced with dignity. "I've always lived here."

"So they grow them crazy here right from the start! Then where's your home you're 'set' to return to?"

"Here in Los."

The girl stood up hastily, a look of alarm on her face.

"Oh, please," Mikel cried, "don't go. I can explain. Perhaps you can help me."

She sat down again dubiously.

"Well, I'm a sucker for a good story," she said. "Shoot."

"I—I wouldn't shoot. I have no weapon."

That wasn't true—he did have a weapon: the knife. But he could hardly mention that. Anyway, the girl only laughed again.

"Wisecracks, yet," she said unintelligibly. "Well, what's the story?"

"I am from this place, but I am not from your time," Mikel began laboriously; he was utterly unaccustomed to social conversation with a woman. "I am from—with me it is 2839."

"What in the—look, what are you advertising? Some science fiction magazine?"

"I don't understand that word—adver—what is it? Please believe me. I shouldn't tell you, I'm breaking a rule. But it is true."

"Go on." She fixed him with a skeptical glance.

"I was—I am a ticket-seller for Time Travel Tours. This morning—I mean what was to me this morning—a customer was killed at my window."

He plunged ahead. She listened in silence, a peculiar expression in her eyes.

"So you see," he concluded, "I am here for a week. But then I go back—the timeporter will see to that. I *want* to go—I'm sorry I ran away. But I'm sure the police will say I did it, because of the knife."

"Let's see it."

He brought it out.

"Why, that's just an ordinary kitchen carving knife," she said, just as the man in the store had done. "I suppose you *would* call it an antique in—what was it?—2839. I still say you're haywire—or else this is some new racket I don't get."

"I don't understand."

"Okay, I guess you wouldn't—in 2839. The language would change plenty in 886 years." Once more her laugh rang out. "I'll say you keep it up fine—that funny half-foreign way you pronounce your words. But I'll play along, and pretend this is all on the up-and-up. Even so, it's haywire—crazy. Because the dumbest cop in the world wouldn't suspect you of the murder. Anybody'd know the murderer just got rid of the knife the quickest way he could. Gosh, you were behind your window, weren't you, and she was in front of it? Where was her stab wound?"

"Wait—it's hard for me to understand. 'Cop'—is that slang for police? And the blood"—he shuddered—"came from her side. Either someone in front or someone behind her could have done it."

"But they'll find out right away, won't they, that you didn't know the girl? They'll find out who she was, and they'll grill everybody she knew, to see who had a reason for wanting her out of the way.... Listen to me! I'm as big a nut as you are. I'm talking just as if the whole thing really happened."

"It did happen," Mikel assured her earnestly. "No, I didn't know her. I don't know any girls at all. I'm—I'm not attractive to women."

"Why, you're not so bad," said the girl kindly. "I think you're kind of cute—or would be, if you weren't rigged up in those outlandish clothes," she paused, then continued, "Well, if you can prove you didn't know her, what have you got to worry about?"

"The knife. And that I lost my head and ran."

•

The girl nodded. "Leave the knife here, then. Or would that change the course of history?" She smiled. "Of course, what you ought to have done was hand it right over. Then if it was such a great antique they'd not only have the guy's fingerprints but they'd also find out who knew her that worked in a museum or had a chance to steal it from one. That's elementary homicide procedure."

"You see," said Mikel, "this also you won't believe. But our police are not conditioned to take care of killings. This is the first time in my whole life that I have ever even heard of one, except by accident. The psychologists wouldn't allow anyone to grow up who had murderous tendencies that couldn't be sublimated."

"They let that one slip by them, didn't they? And do you mean that in the great scientific future they tell us about, the police won't know as much about handling a homicide case as any hick constable knows today? Who're you trying to kid?"

"We do not have crime. The police are to guard traffic and to take up for reconditioning anybody who doesn't obey the civil rules. I don't know much history, but I know there once were wars, and then there were experts in war. Now—in my time—we have no wars, so there are no experts. In the same way we have no experts in crime."

"Then what would they do to you, if they did convict you of this murder you didn't commit?"

"I don't know. There is no penalty for murder because there have been no murders for so long. This will be a world affair; the police will refer it to the Supreme Council, and they will decide what to do. I suppose they will have me euthanized as an atavistic deviant. That's why I lost my head. It was a totally new experience and I haven't been conditioned to new experiences. But even if they don't convict me, they'll punish me for running away. They'll demote me, perhaps all the way back to where I started twelve years ago."

"It doesn't sound like much of a brave new world to me," said the girl in a disparaging tone. "What's your name—or do you just have numbers?"

"My name is Mikel Skot."

"Michael Scott—well, that sounds like a regular name, anyway. Mine's Betty French, by the way."

"Many grats to you, Citizen French. You have given me good advice. I know now it is my duty to take the knife back with me, and give it to the police. I shall tell them also about looking for somebody in a museum, as you suggested. But there will be no fingerprints—I washed the knife in that fountain, when I hoped to sell it. I forgot it *must* exist in my era, or the murder could not have occurred.

"But that is not my big problem now. I have no money of your time. How shall I live until I can go home?"

•

Betty French seemed to stiffen. She looked at him disgustedly. "I get it now," she said. "I might have known. This is just a new way of panhandling. I certainly admire it—it's a work of art. Well, I got my money's worth. I'll pay for it."

She opened her handbag, drew out a dollar bill, and laid it on Mikel's knee. He gazed at it curiously, but made no attempt to pick it up.

"Is that your kind of money?" he asked. "What do I do in exchange for it?"

"Oh, let's drop it," she sighed wearily. "My lunch-hour's up, anyway. Take it—it'll buy you a hamburger and coffee, and then you can tell your tale to the next comer and maybe get enough for a bed in a flophouse. Brother, you must have told it plenty, to get it all down so pat. It's a wonder I've missed you before—or are you just starting to work this neighborhood?"

She snapped her bag shut and stood up.

"Please—I don't understand—why are you so angry?"

At the desperation in his voice she turned and stopped.

"Look—I really have to get back to the office. This *is* an act, isn't it? Come clean—aren't you panhandling?"

"What does 'panhandling' mean?"

"Oh, I give up! I guess you're just looney, after all. All right, Mike, let's call it a day. You keep that buck, and now you just go to the nearest police station and tell them your story. They'll take you over to the psychiatric ward of the county hospital and you can get free board and lodging there."

Mikel turned pale and shivered.

"Oh, no," he breathed. "I'm not insane. If you don't believe me, no one else will. And the hospital will euthanize me."

"Is that what they do to crazy people in—in your time?"

"Of course. And they punish the psychologist who didn't detect the tendency and have the person euthanized in childhood."

"Suppose I give you my word they won't do that to you here and now? They'll just observe you for a few days and then they'll have you committed to a state hospital."

"You are quite positive? If I can be sure of being alive a week from now, no matter where I am, when the timeporter checks I'll go back home."

"Even if you're in a padded cell?"

"It won't matter where."

"Well, then, your problem's solved, isn't it? I'll show you how to get to the station."

"I must eat first. I'm very hungry. And what were those things you said I should get—hamburger and coffee? They are—original foods? Our food is all synthetic."

"You don't have to keep this up with me any more. There's a quick lunch place." She pointed.

"And they won't mind in this Autocaf that I'm not dressed like the others?"

"In this burg? They wouldn't notice if you wandered around in a loincloth. Now I've *got* to go. This is the wackiest thing that ever happened to me, whatever it really means. Well, good luck, Mike!"

"Grats to you, Citizen French, from deep in my pineal. Oh, wait just one min more please!"

"What is it now?"

"You have given me so much to tell our police. But won't they wonder *why* this man killed the girl?"

"They can ask him when they catch them, can't they? But it's perfectly obvious. She was buying a ticket, wasn't she?"

"Yes, certainly."

"Well, that meant she was going away—leaving him, doesn't it? So he was in love with her—maybe she was his wife—and he couldn't take it. Maybe she was going to some other guy—how do I know? He found out she was deserting him, so he got hold of the knife, and followed her."

"But I don't see why." Mikel was utterly bewildered. "She was a free agent, like anybody else. He couldn't object to her leaving if she no longer loved him—he didn't *own* her. That doesn't make sense. If I tell one of our police *that* theory, she will surely think I'm insane."

"She?"

"All our police are women, of course. Women are naturally gifted at keeping order."

"You tell that to our cops, and they'll surely get you tucked away in a nice hospital, but fast. Well, why else *would* he kill her?"

"I don't know. That's why I asked you—you know so much more about such things, in your barb—in your time."

"Your policewoman will have to figure it out for herself. So long, Mike." She shook her head, smiling. "Will I have a tale to tell the crowd—if they don't decide I've gone nuts myself! Good-by!"

"Goobie, Citizen, and grats again."

Still smiling, she hurried down the path out of the park.

●

When he could see her no longer, Mikel stood up and began hesitantly to walk toward the restaurant she had pointed out. Fortunately, it was on the same side of the street, not far past the shop where he tried to sell the knife.

This was not going to be plez, not at all plez. Despite what this Beti French had told him, he was nervous about putting himself in the hands of either the police or psychologist of this barbarous era. But there didn't seem to be anything else he could do. His conversation with the redheaded girl had shown him clearly what kind of reception he would meet from anyone else he ventured to approach.

First he must eat—he was ravenous. He dared not ask for any food except the two things the girl had mentioned, whatever they were like. Presumably the money she had given him would be enough.

The restaurant had a long counter of some white substance, with stools fixed before it. Only one man sat there eating, but behind it stood another man dressed in white, with a white cap on his head. Mikel perched himself on the nearest stool.

"Hamburger, coffee, please," he said, and laid Beti's money beside him on the counter.

The other customer looked up and eyed him sharply, but the man behind the counter merely yelled "One on a bun!" through a hole in the wall. "Mustard?" he asked, "Onions? Cream?"

"No, Citizen. Hamburger, coffee," Mikel repeated, flustered.

"A joker!" the man grunted. "This town! You in the movies, bud?"

Mikel stared.

"He wants a burger without and coffee with," the other customer put in suddenly. He picked up his dishes and slid down to the next stool. He was a heavy-set, middle-aged man, dressed as the man in the store had been—in dark cloth bifurcated leg-coverings and a dark, long-sleeved upper garment over a light-colored under-garment, with a gaudy ribbon around his neck.

"Okay, okay," said the man in white placatingly, and set down before Mikel something on a plate and something else in a cup, both hot. Mikel began sampling them gingerly with the unaccustomed implements. The restaurant man took the money, put it in a box that rang a bell, and laid down some small metal objects in its place. Then he disappeared through a door behind the counter.

Mikel's neighbor waited until he had gone. Then in a low voice he said: "Finish the food, Citizen Skot. Then we'll talk."

Mikel looked up, frozen. The stranger shot his left wrist out from the sleeve. Sealed to it was a timeporter.

"From TTT executive, Citizen," he said briskly. "I didn't think I'd find you quite so soon, but I knew it wouldn't be long, since you didn't wait to get proper equipment for your journey. It is fort for you that this is perhaps the only place in this era where you would not have been taken up at sight for wandering around in unusual clothing."

"How—how did you know what period—"

"We only had to check the tickets, to see which was missing. Have you the knife?"

•

Mikel brought it out dumbly and laid it on the counter. The man put it in a pouch sewed into his lower garment.

"I didn't do it! I didn't!" Mikel cried despairingly. He had lost his appetite completely.

"Sh! We don't want a fuss here. I am rechecking your timeporter, Citizen Skot. We are going back immediately."

"I—I didn't even know the girl!" Mikel pleaded, remembering Beti French's instructions.

"We shall see as to that, when we get home," said the TTT executive grimly.

Then suddenly he burst out laughing. He laughed until he had to take a small piece of white material from his upper garment and wipe his eyes.

"I meant to give you a good scare, to put some sense into you," he gasped finally. "But I can't keep it up. Citizen Skot, you are a fool."

"I know that, Citizen," said Mikel humbly.

"The psychologists really conditioned you a bit too well. I am told that you live for your work and have no recreation at all. You are as ignorant of the world as a small child. Come, did you ever hear of a murder in our time, anywhere, in all your life?"

"No. But I know such things occur."

"In the past, not in our time. How could there be a murder in our era? In the old times, people killed one another for jealousy, for revenge, for greed. Such incentives do not exist in the 29th century. The only other possibility would be insanity, and the psychologists would never allow that to proceed to such a point—the diseased person would be euthanized at the very first symptoms."

"But the girl *was* killed, right before my eyes."

"My poor man, you were a victim of your own ridiculously retired existence. Anyone else would have guessed at once. It was planned that way so as to get a good effect of a crowd in confusion—most of them were extras. Of course all the arrangements had been made with us beforehand, and the concealed telcams were focused away from any Time Travel signs."

"Telecams?"

"World Theater was making a historical crime tridimens in modern dress, Citizen Skot. The girl was an actress. The blood was faked. They thought it would be more effective not to put an actor behind the ticket-window, but to use a real ticket-seller without warning him, just as part of the crowd wasn't warned. It worked beautifully—they tell me your fright and horror showed up wonderfully well.

"They picked your window because they said they liked your looks— I can't imagine why. That was their big mistake. Any other of our ticket-sellers would have waited to see what happened next. You, you dumble, fell into a panic and ran away. And I've had to leave my desk in the middle of a busy aftern to go and fetch you. We couldn't let you wander around here for a week without means of subsistence, and thinking you were suspected of murder!"

"I suppose I'll be demoted now," Mikel said gloomily.

"That wouldn't be fair. This wasn't one of the known responsibilities of your position. No, but I imagine you'll come in for a lot of whiffing, to use a slang expression."

"Kidding—that's what they call it here, I think. Well, I'm used to that."

"And Dafne Dart says she's wild to meet you."

"Dafne Dart? Who's she?" Mikel looked alarmed again.

"Your performance made a tremend impression on her. She told me to tell you she thinks 'you're purely vlumpish.' She's the actress who played the murder victim."

"That red-haired girl with the green eyes with flecks of amber in them?" asked Mikel eagerly. "With the streely smile and the gorge voice?"

"You seem to have noticed her," said the TTT executive dryly. "Yes, that's the one. I thought you didn't go for women."

"But that's different!" Mikel Skot caroled. "Redheads with green eyes—that's the one kind that crashes me and that I crash—I just found it out today.

"Come on, Citizen, what are we waiting for? Let's Go!"

Where the Phph Pebbles Go

Gral and Hodnuth were playing phph. In case you are not a phph fan, and haven't ever seen Bliten's classic *Ways of Improving Your Phph Game*, its essence consists in lobbing pebbles at a target as near the horizon as your skill permits. After each throw, you fly over to see how far you went.

It sounds like a simple game, but it has complicated restrictions and rules, and a good phph player can command any amount of heavy service from the spectators. Since a lot of the Ground Dwellers are also phph addicts (they could never become players, of course, being far too small and light to handle the phph pebbles), this means that a real champion never has to do any kind of work again, being fed, clothed, housed and entertained by his admirers, and can devote all his time to the game.

Gral and Hodnuth, having alternated as champions for many a long ganath, had it pretty easy. But neither of them was given to lying back on his laurels and growing soft. This meant that when a match was announced, Ground Dwellers as well as we Real People came by the hanthoids from zygils around to watch through viewing-tubes—and whichever of the two won piled up a lot of bilibs of voluntary service. (Voluntary service, as most economists admit, is true wealth, since the pledge is incumbent on the offerer's heirs until it is fully satisfied, and can likewise be willed by the recipient to *his* heirs).

Naturally, no phph player is absolutely perfect; if he were, there would be no contest and nobody would bother to attend a game. Pebbles fall short, they go awry, and sometimes they are thrown so hard that they escape altogether from our light gravity and fly into outer space. At the end of the game period the referee (usually a superannuated former champion) tots up the score and announces how many times each player missed the target and by which of these errors he missed it. By a rather confusing arithmetical computation he then determines which of them won, and the winner collects his pledges—and the fans collect the side bets they have been making all through the game.

In this particular game Hodnuth won. But then he won about half the time, so that wasn't what gave it its importance. The Ground Dwellers, as everyone knows, are an excitable and volatile race (which is why we conquered them so easily, with the added advantage of our command of levitation and our immensely greater size and strength), so just an ordinary phph game often looks like a riot. When anything out of the way occurs, such as the appearance of a new young contender to take on one of the champions, the Ground Dwellers simply go wild. And this time they practically exploded. I confess that even we Real People were amazed.

One of the Thinkers was discovered attending the game.

•

Now, when we first arrived here, and cleaned up on the Ground Dwellers and established them in their proper subservient position, the Thinkers were our leaders. It was they who had figured out the whole invasion, had headed the Sixty Hastgunt Flight, and had worked out the tactics and logistics of the Great Conquest. But once we were settled and things were going smoothly, they called a last General Meeting and told us that their part was finished, and that now they were going to retire to the Far Colony and go on with their Thinking. Since then, if a problem arises that our own Council can't handle, one of us has to fly to the Far Colony and obtain the advice of a Thinker. They live together there with their families (supported of course by all of us) and spend all their time in study and research. It is one of the natural advantages of us Real People that we have these specialized Thinkers to do all our intellectual and cultural tasks and teach us what we need to know, leaving us others free for the truly satisfying functions of government and commerce.

Never in all the ganaths since that last General Meeting had a Thinker been seen among us, and that so august a being should condescend to attend a mere phph game was unbelievable. Yet there he was—easily recognizable, naturally, since all Thinkers have long white hair and long white beards. (Even the female Thinkers—though some heretics say their beards are artificial.) In fact, that is the way one knows that a new Thinker has been born. Soon after birth his hair and beard begin to grow, both white, and as soon as he is weaned we fly him to the Far Colony to be reared and educated by his own. If a Thinker has a child who isn't one, they send him back to us.

As soon as the spectators realized that a Thinker was among them, the excitement reached boiling point. The Ground Dwellers almost went crazy—for, of all things, the Thinker had seated himself not in the perches of honor of the Real People, in front, but in the Ground Dwellers' bleachers. We ourselves noticed all the scrambling and heaving, and when some of us flew over to investigate we could hardly believe our eyes.

When I say scrambling and heaving, I don't mean they were mobbing him. They're much too afraid of us for that, and anyway their reverence for the Thinkers is positively religious—much more so than ours. After all the Thinkers are simply specialized members of our own race, and though we revere them we could scarcely worship them, as the Ground Dwellers do. No, they were clearing a respectful space all around him, but then they kept gazing at him in awe, half of them falling on their knees in his presence. I sneaked a glance at the phph players, and as I suspected they were looking anything but happy. Phph champions are pretty vain. They don't care for rival attractions.

One of our party—it was Sephar, who as usual pushed himself forward—bowed to the Thinker and asked if he wouldn't be more comfortable among us. But he shook his white head and said no, he could see better where he was. (I wonder if Thinkers may not have a bit of vanity too, and if he wasn't enjoying seeing all those poor creatures prostrate themselves around him!)

"Then will Your Honor join us when the game is over?" persisted Sephar. "If you would enter my poor pit of a dwelling, it would overwhelm me with pleasure to have you feast with us."

His poor pit of a dwelling, indeed! I wish you could see the palace he lived in—the roof-opening is plated with solid nagh!

•

I was just about bursting with indignation, but I should have known you can trust a Thinker to deflate a fellow like that.

"Thank you, brother," he said mildly, "but I'm here doing some research and I'll have to fly back right after the game."

Sephar opened his mouth to argue, but by that time I had him by the wing and I pulled him back—he said rudely, I say firmly. "Do you want to give us a bad name for presumption, brother?" I whispered. "Don't interfere with a Thinker when he's Thinking!"

Some of the rest of us nodded agreement, so Sephar shut up. But he had a nasty gleam in his eye and I braced myself for trouble later. We bowed and returned to our places. Thanks to Sephar and his performance, I missed the last throw Gral made, which lost him the contest. But I heard the moan from the spectators who weren't watching the Thinker instead, so I knew he'd lobbed a too-high one. It must have been a humdinger—one of the throws into space. I glanced back as I was flying away, and the Thinker was standing up and gazing intently after it. Well, I thought to myself, imagine a Thinker getting worked up over a phph throw!

The game was over soon after that, and Hodnuth went around collecting his pledges while Gral was being consoled by his backers. When I got a chance to look again where the Thinker had been sitting, he had disappeared.

The one who hadn't disappeared was Sephar. He was waiting for me, just as I'd expected.

"Not here!" I snarled at him. "Do you want the Ground Dwellers to see Real People in a brawl?"

So we adjourned to Marnag's courtyard, which was the nearest dueling place, and it was a nice little fight, and I won. Quite a group gathered around, and I was pleased to see that several of my friends were making bets on me. Some of Sephar's sycophants lugged him off to the hospital to have a fractured wing-tip treated. The rest came home with me and we spent our winnings on a good dinner with plenty of mastonyi to wash it down.

Several of us speculated about the Thinker, and we wondered if his "research" wasn't a fake and if he'd just decided to enjoy a game like the rest of us.

"After all," Marnag pointed out, "he might be only a boy. You can't tell with a Thinker. I suppose young Thinkers can be frivolous and rebellious like our own youngsters."

Nipar, who is something of a wag, yelled: "Hey, listen to Marnag—he's Thinking! Come on, Marnag, are you really a Thinker in disguise? Let's see if that green hair of yours is dyed—you could have shaved the beard!"

And he poured a pitcher of mastonyi right over Marnag's head to find out if the color would come off. After that, the party got really rough, and I don't remember the rest of it.

•

A whole ganath after that, the Thinkers sent one of their messengers to tell us in the Council that we were summoned to a meeting in the Far Colony. That doesn't happen often, so we knew something extremely important must be up. I for one was all of a twitter.

Not one of us connected the summons with that Thinker who had come to the phph contest between Gral and Hodnuth. That was our stupidity. We should have guessed it when we found the two champions had been sent for also. Gral flew next to me on the trip, and of all things, both he and Hodnuth were carrying with them several phph pebbles which the Thinkers had ordered them to bring along.

It's hard to tell the Thinkers apart—at least for us who aren't Thinkers—but I recognized the one who had been at the game. He sat right by Hledo, who always acts as their spokesman when we consult them about anything.

"Welcome and thank you for coming so promptly," Hledo began. "Did you two phph players bring the pebbles?"

Gral and Hodnuth handed over the load, and Hledo passed it on to the one we knew.

"This is Myrwan," Hledo said, "and he will tell you the urgent thing he has Thought."

"I became interested a long time ago," Myrwan began in the rather rusty voice all the Thinkers except Hledo have—they spend most of their time in study and meditation, and don't talk much among themselves—"in a question that seems never to have occurred to any of Us.

"Where do phph pebbles go when they are thrown beyond our feeble gravity and escape into outer space? What becomes of them in the end? And who, if anyone, collects them, and what conclusions about them and our world do such persons draw?"

I raised my hand to ask a question, and Myrwan nodded.

"I don't understand." I said politely. (Meaning he was being too abstruse for any of us, for it is understood that there is no keener apprehension in the council than my own.) "Is Your Honor implying that there exist outside our world other intelligences that would be capable of observing and drawing conclusions from the pebbles?"

"Exactly. I know that the general belief is that it is impossible that extraplanetary beings can exist, least of all intelligent beings. That was the belief of my own colleagues until I gave them the results of my recent Thought. It is the reason We have summoned you here.

"For some time now We have been receiving peculiar radio waves from outside the world. We have considered them merely manifestations of random radiation from other planets and stars. But now they have suddenly become—shall I say rhythmical? Measured? Directional? They leave the impression that someone, or something, is trying to communicate with us.

"The astronomers among Us have become more and more concerned. We have finally been led to the reluctant belief that Our former theories have been wrong—that this actually is not the only inhabited planet.

"Now, I need not tell you how disastrous it would be for us if that were true. If there *are* intelligent beings on other planets, if they are trying to communicate with us, then the next step would be that they would try to visit us."

Marnag raised his hand.

"What harm would that do? If such beings exist, and if they could come here, why couldn't we go there too—wherever it is—and wouldn't that enrich our lives? Of course I'm not a Thinker—" I had a fleeting vision of Nipar and the pitcher of mastonyi!—"but I'm a Real Man and I can see no reason why it would hurt us to find we are not alone in the universe."

"No," said Myrwan dryly. "You are not a Thinker, my friend. We enjoy here a completely stable civilization. It is the best of all possible social systems. We do not want it disturbed."

"I see," said Marnag, and several others nodded. I confess that a heretical idea crossed my mind—that any such disturbance might well dethrone the Thinkers first of all—but I suppressed it. Myrwan went on:

"And that is where the phph pebbles come in. In the course of my researches on these previously unknown waves, I began to wonder what, if anything, had initiated the interest of outsiders in our planet, assuming that outsiders exist. Certainly we had made no move toward trying either to reach or to communicate with any putative dwellers on other planets. There had been no major changes on our planet that could have enlisted the attention of outside astronomers, even granting that they have telescopes as powerful as our own.

"Only one thing, so far as I can ascertain, has ever left this planet for outer space. And that was the phph pebbles.

"We call them pebbles. To beings who might consider us giants—and if there really are intelligent beings in other worlds they might well be of an entirely different size from us, though no less dangerous for all that—they might seem huge meteors. Suppose that, though most of them would undoubtedly burn up and all of them be considerably reduced before they struck another planet as meteorites, some of them at least might still be sufficiently large to be analyzed chemically? And suppose that where they struck there existed beings capable of analyzing them?"

•

This was getting a little deep for anybody not a Thinker to take in. Several Council members raised their hands plaintively and so indicated.

"All right, I'll try to make it plainer," Myrwan said. "Let us pretend that instead of the little fragments of space debris that fall harmlessly in the annual meteor showers here, we were pelted with enormous chunks of matter, perhaps causing major damage to property and life. Wouldn't We immediately undertake an intensive study to determine whence they came, and of what, precisely, they consisted?

"And if We found that these residual meteorites contained material indicating their origin in an inhabited world—still worse, in a world sufficiently evolved to entail the possibility or probability that its highest life-forms might be intelligent or even civilized—wouldn't we take steps at once to investigate? Moreover, wouldn't we be outraged to the point where our primary object would be to avenge ourselves?

"Of course we would. And so of course would any beings on other planets, under similar circumstances."

"You mean," Marnag asked, "that if beings came here from space they would attack us?"

"That too. But even if that were not their reaction, curiosity alone could be enough to spur them on to exploration."

"But—but what can we do?" quavered old Gantes. He is really growing too senile to be on the Council much longer.

"We can discourage them. And we can mislead them."

"How?"

"We can make certain that nothing reaches them in the future which gives them the least sign that any but the lowest forms of life, if even those, exist in our world.

"I studied this whole question systematically, as We always do. I came to the conclusion that only the phph pebbles could possibly betray us. I attended a phph game to see for myself if a pebble actually could be thrown with sufficient force to become, as it were, an artificial meteor. I found that it could. Indeed, I saw Gral make such a throw."

Gral looked stricken. He fell flat on his face, groveling before the Thinkers.

"Oh, Your Reverences," he cried, "I never dreamt—I never—"

"Get up, Gral," Myrwan ordered. "Nobody's blaming you. Nobody expects anyone but a Thinker to Think."

"We'll make it a rule from now on to hold our shots. We'll bar anyone from the game forever who lobs a pebble too hard," Hodnuth promised fervently.

"Far from it," said Myrwan. "On the contrary, in the future you must concentrate on supra-gravity shots. Give extra points to anyone who performs one."

"Why?" several of us murmured, completely bewildered.

"Because I have already analyzed three pebbles I brought back with me from the game. With the ones you have brought, I shall be able to make further tests. If they confirm my previous findings, I Think We shall be able to mislead any potential attackers.

"Every phph pebble henceforth will be doctored. To use any unauthorized pebble will become a felony. What has happened in the past we can't change, but there may still be time to save ourselves. From this time forth there are going to be more 'meteors' shot off our atmosphere than ever before—and every one of them is going to tell a completely false story about conditions in their place of origin.

"Of course We *may* be entirely wrong. These new waves may be due to purely physical causes. Other planets may all be as devoid of intelligent life as We have always assumed. But if there is the faintest possibility—and I feel there is—that we are in danger, it would be fatal not to take such measures as we can to avert it."

"What's in the pebbles now that could tell anything about us?" Gral asked. "And if something is, how could you alter it?"

•

Myrwan froze up a little. The Thinkers don't like to have us ask detailed questions. But he realized that Gral was still upset, and answered kindly.

"It wouldn't mean a lot to you if I told you. But you can understand this much—chemical analysis of the pebbles I've looked at so far shows fragments of embedded fossils."

"Of plants, you mean?"

Myrwan smiled.

"Plants don't become fossilized," he said. "In one pebble there was a microscopic piece of a metal knife. In another there was half of a fossilized tooth. Ground Dweller relics, true, but human. You must remember that all the hills around here from which you gather the pebbles are really million-ganath-old burial places of the Ground Dwellers. We haven't bothered to dig up most of them because we're so rich in prehistoric remains, with our immensely old civilization, that we have all the fossils and ancient artifacts we need.

"But let's imagine an alien civilization a great deal younger than ours. Let's imagine that in even one of those pebbles—which would be meteorites to them—even a minute trace of that kind of thing should be left. What would they Think?—for they would have to have Thinkers too, to be civilized at all.

"I'll tell you what they'd Think. They'd decide that somewhere out in space there is a rich, undiscovered planet full of valuable knowledge and, even better, valuable artifacts. Probably a world with a culture much more advanced than their own. And they'd try hard to trace the direction from which those meteorites came, and to calculate the distance. Then suppose they had some means of transportation in space.

"*That* may well be what these new radio waves mean. They may be attempts at communication—if we were foolish enough to respond to them. We don't dare to take any chances.

"So from now on there are going to be swarms and swarms of those meteoroids—and every one of them is going to be a real artifact on its own—a *manufactured* one, made according to Our specifications, carrying an unmistakable message. A false one!

"They will be cunningly constructed from forms of matter injurious to any conceivable variety of life. We'll cover them all. And they'll be barren of even the most primitive bacteria. They will carry in themselves a silent warning: 'Approach the planet from which these come at peril of your instant death ... no matter what kind of being you are!' That should save us forever."

I'd been wondering why Sephar had kept his big mouth shut all this time. To my way of feeling, he should never have been with us at all. He would never have been a Council member if he hadn't been a multibilibaire. But I'd won a fair fight with him, and officially we had to be friends, so I hadn't protested when I found he was included in the summons.

But now the big blowhard had to put his two grocs' worth.
"Your Reverence—Your Honor—" he spluttered. "May I ask a question?"

"Certainly, brother."

"Since players have been lobbing pebbles out into space for thousands and thousands of ganaths, and as Your Honor says, some of them must long ago have landed somewhere, who knows what dead give-aways may have been in any of them?"

"Is that your question?"

"No, I have two. First, why haven't these intelligent beings whose existence you're presupposing—" I saw Myrwan's face set, and I knew he'd noted that rude and insulting word, but I managed to conceal my smile—"why haven't they come here before this? And since they haven't come, if they're smart enough to figure out our whereabouts why aren't they also smart enough to realize the difference between the old pebbles and these new ones, and to know that we're putting something over on them?"

We sometimes say that though the Thinkers are of course overwhelmingly our superiors mentally, they lack the emotional control which is the great characteristic of the rest of us Real People. I wish those scandalmongers could have seen Myrwan then. His face was as white as his beard and his wings quivered, but he let Sephar have his say out and he answered him very quietly.

"As to your first question, brother," (and if anybody ever called me "brother" in that tone I'd know it was a case of fight or run) "the only logical reason is that it must be only recently that such beings have reached a state of culture where they are able to analyze the pebbles and draw the right conclusions from them.

"And the answer to your second question is that we can only hope. Hope that all of the pebbles already in their possession are free of—shall we say, incriminating evidence? All we can guarantee is that all they find in the future will be. Does that answer you satisfactorily?"

"It will have to," muttered Sephar sullenly. I moved away from him and was glad to notice that I was not the only one.

"What I have said to you," continued the Thinker calmly, "you may communicate to any of the Real People you wish. You will naturally keep it from the Ground Dwellers; there is no reason to agitate them at present. Time enough for that if we should ever need them as soldiers— which I devoutly hope we never shall."

"But who will make the artificial pebbles if the Ground Dwellers aren't to know about them?" asked Marnag. "What about our slogan— 'Thought from the Thinkers, government and administration from the Real People, technical skill and heavy labor from the Ground Dwellers'?"

"*We* shall handle that. When you go home, tell Earnig I want to see him at once. Brief him first. He and his Bureau will see that the job is done, and the Ground Dwellers needn't be told just what they are making. They'll be delighted to hear that We are planning a new kind of phph pebble to increase the interest of the game—they love it whenever one is batted clear away."

•

Well, all this was last ganath. The new pebbles are in use. So far nothing has happened—unless you count the fact that, according to Myrwan, those peculiar radio waves have ceased. Let us hope that if his whole theory is correct—and Thinkers don't talk about their Thoughts till they're pretty sure of them—those alien beings have given up, decided either that they were mistaken and there is no intelligence here able to communicate, or that they themselves haven't the ability to interpret our answers.

Sephar? Oh, he isn't around any more. One of the Thinkers is doing some experiments in Psychological Adjustment. Hledo asked the Council's recommendation of somebody they could commandeer as a test subject, according to the Agreement on Thinkers' Privileges, and I got them to suggest Sephar. He was very nasty about it, but I ignored his underbred invective. I felt it my duty also respectfully to remind Hledo of Sephar's past indiscretions, in case they'd forgotten.

Usually when the Thinkers have finished with a subject he's no longer of much use and they put him in a rest home for the remainder of his life. So since I've done pretty well for myself lately, I was able to buy Sephar's home, with its nagh-plated roof-opening, and move into it.

He had a very attractive wife, who of course couldn't go with him to the Far Colony. It just goes to show that virtue (as one of the Thinkers once remarked wittily) is its own reward.

The Eel

He was intimately and unfavorably known everywhere in the Galaxy, but with special virulence on eight planets in three different solar systems. He was eagerly sought on each; they all wanted to try him and punish him—in each case, by their own laws and customs. This had been going on for 26 terrestrial years, which means from minus ten to plus 280 in some of the others. The only place that didn't want him was Earth, his native planet, where he was too smart to operate—but, of course, the Galactic Police were looking for him there too, to deliver him to the authorities of the other planets in accordance with the Interplanetary Constitution.

For all of those years, The Eel (which was his Earth monicker; elsewhere, he was known by names indicating equally squirmy and slimy life-forms) had been gayly going his way, known under a dozen different aliases, turning up suddenly here, there, everywhere, committing his gigantic depredations, and disappearing as quickly and silently when his latest enterprise had succeeded. He specialized in enormous, unprecedented thefts. It was said that he despised stealing anything under the value of 100 million terrestrial units, and most of his thefts were much larger than that.

He had no recognizable *modus operandi*, changing his methods with each new crime. He never left a clue. But, in bravado, he signed his name to every job: his monicker flattered him, and after each malefaction the victim—usually a government agency, a giant corporation, or one of the clan enterprises of the smaller planets—would receive a message consisting merely of the impudent depiction of a large wriggling eel.

They got him at last, of course. The Galactic Police, like the prehistoric Royal Canadian Mounted, have the reputation of always catching their man. (Sometimes they don't catch him till he's dead, but they catch him.) It took them 26 years, and it was a hard job, for The Eel always worked alone and never talked afterward.

They did it by the herculean labor of investigating the source of the fortune of every inhabitant of Earth, since all that was known was that The Eel was a terrestrial. Every computer in the Federation worked overtime analyzing the data fed into it. It wasn't entirely a thankless task, for, as a by-product, a lot of embezzlers, tax evaders and lesser robbers were turned up.

In the end, it narrowed down to one man who owned more than he could account for having. Even so, they almost lost him, for his takings were cached away under so many pseudonyms that it took several months just to establish that they all belonged to the same person. When that was settled, the police swooped. The Eel surrendered quietly; the one thing he had been surest of was never being apprehended, and he was so dumfounded he was unable to put up any resistance.

And then came the still greater question: which of the planets was to have him?

•

Xystil said it had the first right because his theft there had been the largest—a sum so huge, it could be expressed only by an algebraic index. Artha's argument was that his first recorded crime had been on that planet. Medoris wanted him because its only penalty for any felony is an immediate and rather horrible death, and that would guarantee getting rid of The Eel forever.

Ceres put in a claim on the ground that it was the only planet or moon in the Sol System in which he had operated, and since he was a terrestrial, it was a matter for local jurisdiction. Eb pleaded that it was the newest and poorest member of the Galactic Federation, and should have been protected in its inexperience against his thievishness.

Ha-Almirath argued that it had earned his custody because it was its Chief Ruler who had suggested to the police the method which had resulted in his arrest. Vavinour countered that it should be the chosen recipient, since the theft there had included desecration of the High Temple.

Little Agsk, which was only a probationary Galactic Associate, modestly said that if it were given The Eel, its prompt and exemplary punishment might qualify it for full membership, and it would be grateful for the chance.

A special meeting of the Galactic Council had to be called for the sole purpose of deciding who got The Eel.

Representatives of all the claimant planets made their representations. Each told in eloquent detail why his planet and his alone was entitled to custody of the arch-criminal, and what they would do to him when—not if—they got him. After they had all been heard, the councilors went into executive session, with press and public barred. An indiscreet councilor (it was O-Al of Phlagon of Altair, if you want to know) leaked later some of the rather indecorous proceedings.

The Earth councilor, he reported, had been granted a voice but no vote, since Earth was not an interested party as to the crime, but only as to the criminal. Every possible system of arbitration had been discussed—chronological, numerical in respect to the size of the theft, legalistic in respect to whether the culprit would be available to hand on to another victim when the first had got through punishing him.

In the welter of claims and counterclaims, one harassed councilor wearily suggested a lottery. Another in desperation recommended handing The Eel a list of prospective punishments on each of the eight planets and observing which one seemed to inspire him with most dread—which would then be the one selected. One even proposed poisoning him and announcing his sudden collapse and death.

The sessions went on day and night; the exhausted councilors separated for brief periods of sleep, then went at it again. A hung jury was unthinkable; something had to be decided. The news outlets of the entire Galaxy were beginning to issue sarcastic editorials about procrastination and coddling criminals, with hints about bribery and corruption, and remarks that perhaps what was needed was a few impeachments and a new general election.

So at last, in utter despair, they awarded The Eel to Agsk, as a sort of bonus and incentive. Whichever planet they named, the other seven were going to scream to high heaven, and Agsk was least likely to be able to retaliate against any expressions of indignation.

•

Agskians, as everyone knows, are fairly humanoid beings, primitives from the outer edge of the Galaxy. They were like college freshmen invited to a senior fraternity. This was their Big Chance to Make Good. The Eel, taciturn as ever, was delivered to a delegation of six of them sent to meet him in one of their lumbering spaceships, a low countergrav machine such as Earth had outgrown several millennia before. They were so afraid of losing him that they put a metal belt around him with six chains attached to it, and fastened all six of themselves to him. Once on Agsk, he was placed in a specially made stone pit, surrounded by guards, and fed through the only opening.

In preparation for the influx of visitors to the trial, an anticipated greater assembly of off-planeters than little Agsk had ever seen, they evacuated their capital city temporarily, resettling all its citizens except those needed to serve and care for the guests, and remodeled the biggest houses for the accommodation of those who had peculiar space, shape, or other requirements.

Never since the Galactic Federation was founded had so many beings, human, humanoid, semi-humanoid and non-humanoid, gathered at the same time on any one member-planet. Every newstape, tridimens, audio and all other varieties of information services—even including the drum amplifiers of Medoris and the ray-variants of Eb—applied for and were granted a place in the courtroom. This, because no other edifice was large enough, was an immense stone amphitheater usually devoted to rather curious games with animals; since it rains on Agsk only for two specified hours on every one of their days, no roof was needed. At every seat, there was a translatophone, with interpreters ready in plastic cages to translate the Intergalactic in which the trial was conducted into even the clicks and hisses of Jorg and the eye-flashes of Omonro.

And in the midst of all this, the cause and purpose of it all, sat the legendary Eel.

Seen at last, he was hardly an impressive figure. Time had been going on and The Eel was in his fifties, bald and a trifle paunchy. He was completely ordinary in appearance, a circumstance which had, of course, enabled him to pass unobserved on so many planets; he looked like a salesman or a minor official, and had indeed been so taken by the unnoticing inhabitants of innumerable planets.

People had wondered, when word came of some new outrage by this master-thief, if perhaps he had disguised himself as a resident of the scene of each fresh crime, but now it was obvious that this had not been necessary. He had been too clever to pick any planet where visitors from Earth were not a common sight, and he had been too insignificant for anyone to pay attention to him.

•

The criminal code of Agsk is unique in the Galaxy, though there are rumors of something similar among a legendary extinct tribe on Earth called the Guanches. The high priest is also the chief executive (as well as the minister of education and head of the medical faculty), and he rules jointly with a priestess who also officiates as chief judge.

The Agskians have some strange ideas to a terrestrial eye—for example, suicide is an honor, and anyone of insufficient rank who commits it condemns his immediate family to punishment for his presumption. They are great family people, in general. Also, they never lie, and find it hard to realize that other beings do.

Murder, to them, is merely a matter for negotiation between the murderer and the relatives of the victim, provided it is open and without deceit. But grand larceny, since property is the foundation of the family, is punished in a way that shows that the Agskians, though technologically primitive, are psychologically very advanced.

They reason that death, because it comes inevitably to all, is the least of misfortunes. Lasting grief, remorse and guilt are the greatest. So they let the thief live and do not even imprison him.

Instead, they find out who it is that the criminal most loves. If they do not know who it is, they merely ask him, and since Agskians never lie, he always tells them. Then they seize that person, and kill him or her, slowly and painfully, before the thief's eyes.

And the agreement had been that The Eel was to be tried and punished by the laws and customs of the planet to which he was awarded.

The actual trial and conviction of The Eel were almost perfunctory. Without needing to resort to torture, his jailers had been presented, on a platter as it were, with a full confession—so far as the particular robbery he had committed on Agsk was concerned. There is a provision for defense in the Agskian code, but it was unneeded because The Eel had pleaded guilty.

But he knew very well he would not be executed by the Agskians; he would instead be set free (presumably with a broken heart) to be handed over to the next claimant—and that, the Council had decided, would be Medoris. Since Medoris always kills its criminals, that would end the whole controversy.

So The Eel was quite aware that his conviction by Agsk would be only the preliminary to an exquisitely painful and lingering demise at the two-clawed hands of the Medorans. His business was somehow to get out from under.

Naturally, the resources of the Galactic Police had been at the full disposal of the officials of Agsk.

The files had been opened, and the Agskians had before them The Eel's history back to the day of his birth. He himself had been questioned, encelographed, hypnotized, dormitized, injected, psychographed, subjected to all the means of eliciting information devised by all eight planets—for the other seven, once their first resentment was over, had reconciled themselves and cooperated whole-heartedly with Agsk. Medoris especially had been of the greatest help. The Medorans could hardly wait.

•

In the spate of news of the trial that inundated every portion of the Galaxy, there began to be discovered a note of sympathy for this one little creature arrayed against the mightiest powers of the Galaxy. Poor people who wished they had his nerve, and romantic people who dreamed of adventures they would never dare perform, began to say that The Eel wasn't so bad, after all; he became a symbol of the rebellious individual thumbing his nose at entrenched authority. Students of Earth prehistory will recognize such symbols in the mythical Robin Hood and Al Capone.

These were the people who were glad to put up when bets began to be made. At first the odds were ten to one against The Eel; then, as time dragged by, they dropped until it was even money.

Agsk itself began to be worried. It was one thing to make a big, expensive splurge to impress the Galaxy and to hasten its acceptance into full membership in the Federation, but nobody had expected the show to last more than a few days. If it kept on much longer, Agsk would be bankrupt.

For the trial had foundered on one insoluble problem: the only way The Eel could ever be punished by their laws was to kill the person he most loved—and nobody could discover that he had ever loved anybody.

His mother? His father? He had been an undutiful and unaffectionate son, and his parents were long since dead in any case. He had never had a brother, a sister, a wife or a child. No probing could find any woman with whom he had ever been in love. He had never had an intimate friend.

He did nothing to help, naturally. He simply sat in his chains and smiled and waited. He was perfectly willing to be escorted from the court every evening, relieved of his fetters and placed in his pit. It was a much pleasanter existence than being executed inch by inch by the Medorans. For all he cared, the Agskians could go on spending their planetary income until he finally died of old age.

The priestess-judge and her co-adjutors wore themselves out in discussions far into the night. They lost up to 15 pounds apiece, which on Agsk, where the average weight of adults is about 40, was serious. It began to look as if The Eel's judges would predecease him.

Whom did The Eel love? They went into minutiae and subterfuges. He had never had a pet to which he was devoted. He had never even loved a house which could be razed. He could not be said to have loved the immense fortune he had stolen, for he had concealed his wealth and used little of it, and in any event it had all been confiscated and, so far as possible, restored proportionately to those he had robbed.

What he had loved most, doubtless, was his prowess in stealing unimaginable sums and getting away with it—but there is no way of "killing" a criminal technique.

•

Almost a year had passed. Agsk was beginning to wish The Eel had never been caught, or that they had never been awarded the glory of trying him.

At last the priestess-judge, in utter despair, took off her judge's robes, put on the cassock and surplice of her sacred calling, and laid the problem before the most unapproachable and august of the gods of Agsk.

The trial was suspended while she lay for three days in a trance on the high altar. She emerged weak and tottering, her skin light blue instead of its healthy purple, but her head high and her mouth curved in triumph. At sight of her, renewed excitement surged through the audience. News-gatherers, who had been finding it difficult of late to get anything to report, rushed to their instruments.

"Remove the defendant's chains and set him free," the priestess-judge ordered in ringing tones. "The Great God of the Unspeakable Name has revealed to me whom the defendant most loves. As soon as he is freed, seize him and slay him. For the only being he loves is—himself."

There was an instant's silence, and then a roar. The Medorans howled in frustration.

But The Eel, still guarded but unchained, stood up and laughed aloud.

"Your Great God is a fool!" he said blasphemously. "I deny that I love myself. I care nothing for myself at all."

The priestess-judge sighed. "Since this is your sworn denial, it must be true," she said. "So then we cannot kill you. Instead, we grant that you do indeed love no one. Therefore you are a creature so far outside our comprehension that you cannot come under our laws, no matter how you have broken them. We shall notify the Federation that we abandon our jurisdiction and hand you over to our sister-planet which is next in line to judge you."

Then all the viewers on tridimens on countless planets saw something that nobody had ever thought to see—The Eel's armor of self-confidence cracked and terror poured through the gap.

He dropped to his knees and cried: "Wait! Wait! I confess that I blasphemed your god, but without realizing that I did!"

"You mean," pressed the priestess-judge, "you acknowledge that you yourself are the only being dear to you?"

"No, not that, either. Until now, I have never known love. But now it has come upon me like a nova and I must speak the truth." He paused, still on his knees, and looked piteously at the priestess-judge. "Are—are you bound by your law to—to believe me and to kill, instead of me, this—this being I adore?"

"We are so bound," she stated.

"Then," said The Eel, smiling and confident again, rising to his feet, "before all the Galaxy, I must declare the object of my sudden but everlasting passion. Great lady, it is you!"

•

The Eel is still in his pit, which has been made most comfortable by his sympathizers, while the Council of the Galactic Federation seeks feverishly and vainly, year after year, to find some legal way out of the impasse.

Agsk, however, requests all Federation citizens to submit solutions, the grand prize for a workable answer being a lifetime term as president of the planet. A secondary contest (prize: lifetime ambassadorship to the Galactic Federation) is offered for a legal way around the statute barring criminals (specifically The Eel) from entering the primary contest.

Acknowledgements

Not Snow, Nor Rain - first appeared in Worlds of If, November 1959 - Illustrator: Ed Emshwiller

Oh, Rats! - first appeared in Galaxy Magazine, December 1961 - Illustrator: Wallace Wood

One Way - first appeared in Galaxy Magazine, March 1955 - Illustrator: Irv Docktor

The Margenes - first appeared in Worlds of If, February 1956

The Akkra Case - first appeared in Amazing Stories, January 1962 - Illustrator: Dan Adkins

Time Out for Redheads - first appeared in Startling Stories, Summer 1955 - Illustrator: Kelly Freas

Where the Phph Pebbles Go - first appeared in Worlds of Tomorrow, April 1963 - Illustrator: John Pederson

The Eel - first appeared in Galaxy Magazine, April 1958 - Illustrator: Diane Dillon & Leo Dillon

SPACE
COWBOY

www.ingramcontent.com/pod-product-compliance
Lightning Source LLC
Chambersburg PA
CBHW010729310726
48971CB00009B/2784